Spell & Spindle

ALSO BY MICHELLE SCHUSTERMAN

Olive and the Backstage Ghost

I HEART BAND SERIES
I Heart Band
Friends, Fugues, and Fortune Cookies
Sleepovers, Solos, and Sheet Music
Crushes, Codas, and Corsages

THE KAT SINCLAIR FILES
Dead Air
Graveyard Slot
Final Girl

Spell & Spindle

MICHELLE SCHUSTERMAN

ILLUSTRATIONS BY KATHRIN HONESTA

Random House 🏠 New York

This is a work of fiction. Names, characters, places, and incidents either are the product of the author's imagination or are used fictitiously. Any resemblance to actual persons, living or dead, events, or locales is entirely coincidental.

Text copyright © 2018 by Michelle Schusterman
Jacket art and interior illustrations copyright © 2018 by Kathrin Honesta

Visit us on the Web! rhcbooks.com

"Pennies From Heaven" Words by JOHNNY BURKE
Music by ARTHUR JOHNSTON © 1936 (Renewed) CHAPPEL & CO., INC.
All rights reserved. Used by permission of ALFRED PUBLISHING, LLC

Educators and librarians, for a variety of teaching tools,
visit us at RHTeachersLibrarians.com

Library of Congress Cataloging-in-Publication Data
Name: Schusterman, Michelle, author.
Title: Spell and spindle / by Michelle Schusterman ; illustrations by Kathrin Honesta.
Description: First edition. | New York : Random House, [2018] |
Summary: Eleven-year-old Chance accidentally helps Penny, a lonely marionette who cannot remember who she is or where she came from, discover the truth of her past.
Identifiers: LCCN 2016039741 | ISBN 978-0-399-55070-6 (hardcover) |
ISBN 978-0-399-55071-3 (hardcover library binding) | ISBN 978-0-399-55072-0 (ebook)
Subjects: | CYAC: Marionettes—Fiction. Puppets—Fiction.
Classification: LCC PZ7.S39834 Sp 2018 | DDC [Fic]—dc23

Printed in the United States of America
10 9 8 7 6 5 4 3 2 1
First Edition

For the pessimists, who were right all along

CONTENTS

Prologue: The Cabinetmaker's Apprentice   1

1. A Storm Is Brewing   5

2. A Practical Puppet   11

3. The Soul-Stealing Type   17

4. Fish Face   24

5. A Boy Puppet   33

6. Nothing   42

7. A Mysterious Package from an Enemy   45

8. A Spindle from a Spinning Wheel   55

9. A Hero   63

10. Mopping   65

11. The Puppeteer   71

12. Ready for an Adventure   78

13. Endless Patience   92

14. A Wonderful Big Sister   96

15. A Much Better Match   108

16. A Little Risk   117

17. Spinning   127

18. Lost Soul   131

19. Not Déjà Vu   137

20. The Soul Inside the Princess   147

21. A Familiar Stranger   153

22. The Brave Knight   159

23. Missing   163

24. Something from Nothing   170

25. The Storm   175

26. The First Step   182

27. Her Puppet Shell   185

28. Hope   192

29. An Amazing Sense to Possess   197

30. Obviously a Trap   201

31. The Cabinetmaker's Legendary Chambers   207

32. The Real Story   211

33. Unraveling   217

34. Hollow Wooden Girl   227

35. Nicolette   233

36. *Thump-Thump*   238

37. Somewhere in That Fog   245

38. Enough Happy Endings   249

Spell & Spindle

THE CABINETMAKER'S APPRENTICE

There was once a cabinetmaker's apprentice who built a marionette, and this marionette was not a soul-thieving demon.

Not at first.

The apprentice was an exceptionally talented woodworker, perhaps even more so than the cabinetmaker himself. But he was a lonely young boy, and as it does in so many stories, loneliness led to trouble.

He knew the cabinetmaker's tools were enchanted with some strange magic. That was, after all, how the old man built such extraordinary cabinets. But the apprentice believed the tools might be used to build something even more extraordinary. Something right out of a fairy tale.

A life-size puppet so lifelike it was almost real.

He stole his master's magical tools and set to work, carving and sculpting the wood, painting the face, painstakingly sewing hair strand by strand. When he finished, he stepped back to admire his handiwork. His marionette was a girl, and a very pretty one at that.

The apprentice stared into her glass eyes, amazed. She looked so alive.

The marionette stared back at the boy, equally amazed. He *was* so alive.

Something sparked inside her hollow wooden body. Envy, dark and wicked.

I'm so sad, she told the apprentice, her voice hypnotically sweet. *I wish I had a soul like yours, a soul to make me truly alive instead of just lifelike. Wouldn't that be wonderful?*

The apprentice agreed that, yes, it would be more than wonderful, for at last he would have a real friend. But no magical tool, no trick of the trade, nothing existed to help him create an actual soul. That did not stop him from trying, and the deeper he fell under the spell of this demon he had created, the more desperate his efforts became.

You cannot create a soul for me, the marionette said at last. *But you can give me one. Will you?*

The poor boy was so entranced by this soulless demon, he did not hesitate to reply.

"Yes," he said, and he took up the cabinetmaker's magical tools once more.

He would take out his own soul and give it to his pretty marionette. He just had to figure out how.

A STORM IS BREWING

Just one block from the west lawn of the city's largest park stood an unusual museum. In the many decades it had called this spot home, it had changed names frequently. Some of the city's residents remembered it as the Miracle Rooms. A few elderly citizens swore it had been called the Memory Theater, while others argued it was actually the Hall of Wonders.

Its original owner was a famed cabinetmaker, a man rumored to have had the ability to draw magic from wood. He was said to have built one particularly magical cabinet to house all the others: chambers of infinite cabinets filled with his legendary collection of curiosities. The cabinet containing the chambers had been lost in the great fire that devoured much of the city half a century ago, but old-timers could often be heard spinning yarns about its vastness:

"It was a beautiful oak cabinet, and inside was an endless maze of cabinets, all filled with the most bizarre things you'd ever laid eyes on."

"Open one and you might find a display of Minotaur horns or scraps of wood from the Trojan horse. Open another and you'd be looking at a genuine fairy skeleton!"

"I was too young to remember, but my granddaddy said he was lost in there for weeks—ate his own socks before he found his way out!"

Nowadays the little museum housed all that remained of the cabinetmaker's collection. While children still listened with starry eyes to the tales of its former grandeur, adults merely shook their heads with a mixture of amusement and distaste. Because in this modern age, such dusty old artifacts were called "oddities" at best, and "horrors" at worst. As a compromise, the institution now bore the somewhat sardonic title of the Museum of the Peculiar Arts. But it wouldn't for much longer, as it had recently been sold, and the new owner had other plans for the building.

An elderly man named Fortunato had inherited the museum from the cabinetmaker. Fortunato had been orphaned at a young age, and the old cabinetmaker had taken him in. Selling the museum had broken Fortunato's heart, as it was all he had left of the man he'd called Papa.

Back when the city had been weak and struggling, poor citizens had been happy to drop a few coins for any form of entertainment. But one great war later, the city was different—a prosperous, booming beast, its ego constantly fed and fueled by its inhabitants, making it more glamorous (and more ghastly) than ever. Few were interested in spending their leisure time inspecting dusty oddities and cursed relics.

Fortunato lived above the museum, on the second floor. The Bonvillain family lived on the floor above him. Mr. Bonvillain was the museum's accountant, and when Fortunato informed him the place was closing, he waited until the poor old man was out of sight before dancing a little jig. Mr. Bonvillain felt certain this was a sign that there was something better out there for him. And sure enough, within a week he landed a job at a brand-new bank in the shiny financial district and immediately bought a brand-new house in the suburbs to match. It was, he and his wife told their children, an opportunity to "move up in the world."

Constance, his perpetually cheerful thirteen-year-old daughter, agreed. Like her parents, she believed all change could be good so long as you stayed positive about it. And besides, she had been raised to be an obedient young lady who always expressed agreement with her mouth, even if her brain and heart felt otherwise.

Eleven-year-old Chance was another story. He found his family's relentless optimism to be a real downer. The suburbs sounded boring beyond belief, the opposite setting for the kind of action and adventure his heroes from comic books and television and radio experienced. He dreaded the thought of giving up his after-school job as Fortunato's apprentice for something dull, like mowing lawns. Who in their right mind could possibly prefer pulling weeds in some stupid flower garden to handling fantastically grotesque and potentially dangerous objects in the quiet dark of a museum?

But Chance thought his father was right about one thing: the closing of the Museum of the Peculiar Arts *was* an opportunity.

An opportunity for Chance to finally have a real adventure of his own.

A natural-born pessimist, Chance was greatly misunderstood by his family, who had spent his entire life trying to cheer him up. They mistook his pessimism for sadness or anger. But really Chance was just preparing for the worst. Because at some point, he figured, the worst was bound to come for you.

Exactly one week before the big move, Chance turned on the family's old radio and waited for his favorite program. The Bonvillains had a television, too, but Chance preferred imagining scenes playing out in his mind as he listened. Constance sat cross-legged on the carpet next to him, a brochure opened in her lap. *Welcome to Daystar Meadows,* it read over a photo of a smiling family of four standing in front of a blue house with white trim. *Opening Summer 1952!*

"We'll have a backyard," Constance said, turning the page. "I could plant a garden. Ooh, look at those white picket fences—perfect for rosebushes!"

Chance squinted at a photo of a street. "The houses all look the same."

"Not exactly," Constance pointed out. "The paint jobs are different. Dad says ours is yellow."

"So when it gets egged, it'll blend in?"

His sister giggled. Chance's parents found his constant negativity worrisome, but Constance seemed to love him all the more for it. She was a good sister, he thought, though exhaustingly upbeat.

Constance flipped back to the picture of an empty grass lawn and started to list all the possibilities: a garden, a swing set, a pool. But Chance didn't see what was so great about a backyard when you could have an entire city as your playground.

"A storm is brewing," a crackly voice came through the radio speakers, and Chance hastily turned up the volume. *"Are YOU prepared for the worst?"*

Constance fell silent at once and closed the pamphlet. *Storm at Dawn* was a popular program, and Chance's favorite. Most listeners—like Constance—found the Storm's constant doomsday warnings to be more amusing than ominous. Chance, on the other hand, thought the character was wiser and braver than anyone he'd ever met in real life. He felt a deep kinship with the Storm and took every episode very seriously.

"*Last time on* Storm at Dawn, *our fearless and mysterious hero, known only as the Storm, a man possessing the terrible gift of premonition, found himself once again in the face of grave danger as he fell under the hypnotic powers of his archenemy, Madam M, who was desperate to steal the Storm's powers for herself. . . .*"

Chance leaned forward, listening intently. He had learned a lot from the Storm about what to do in dangerous situations, and he needed all the help he could get. Because in one week the Bonvillains were moving to Daystar Meadows. But Chance was not going with them.

He had bigger plans.

A PRACTICAL PUPPET

As a marionette, Penny had a bird's-eye view of the interior of the Museum of the Peculiar Arts. She had sat on the top shelf of her curio cabinet for as long as she could remember, back to back with her own reflection, overlooking the maze of glass tables and shelves. She had long memorized the position of each and every oddity.

The surface of the high ceiling was covered with mounted fossils: glimmering fish and delicate birds, pearly shells and bright corals, even an enormous crocodile, tail curved and mouth agape to show off rows of razor-sharp teeth. All the curio cabinets lining the walls were mirrored, as were the glass tables and shelves taking up much of the floor space, which gave the impression of an infinitely larger collection. There was a healthy mix of phony items with the real ones, though Penny suspected that Fortunato believed each to be genuine: the stuffed phoenix with its blood-red feathers, the locked case of unicorn horns and narwhal tusks, the preserved skeleton of what appeared to be a tiny fairy, its wing bones as fine as hair. The black pearl necklace said to darken the soul of its wearer often attracted the most attention from visitors, while the ancient diary bound in its former owner's skin, with a lock made of jawbone and teeth, caused most to recoil in disgust.

Penny's favorite curiosity was the functional mechanical heart that whistled and ticked and sped up when touched. She would stare at it for hours on end, imagining what it would feel like inside her chest.

Penny had only ever moved once, at least that she could clearly recall. Years ago a young museum visitor had stood on tiptoes to squint up at her.

"'Penny,'" she'd read, and that had been the moment when Penny realized there was a label bearing her name on the shelf. Then the girl had reached for Penny, accidentally knocking her off.

The ensuing free fall had been a thrilling few seconds. At least, Penny was sure she would have found it thrilling if she were capable of experiencing emotions. She had hit the floor in a clatter of wooden limbs, and Fortunato had cried:

"Nicolette!"

He'd scooped Penny up, examining her closely for signs of new damage. The flustered little girl, after apologizing, had hesitantly pointed out that her label said PENNY, not NICOLETTE.

Fortunato's expression had gone odd. "Her name *is* Penny," he had told the girl, placing Penny back on her shelf. "I misspoke. Here, have you seen the cursed necklace yet?"

He'd led the girl off, neither of them looking back at Penny.

She had held the name Nicolette in her mind ever since. Why had Fortunato called her that? Could there have been another life-size, lifelike marionette? What had happened to her? Something dreadful, surely.

Perhaps Penny had once known who Nicolette was. Perhaps Penny had known a lot of things once. Fog clouded her memories from before the museum, and she only caught them in glimpses here and there: a stage, a deep red curtain, long-fingered hands gripping her strings and making her dance. Penny loved to think about dancing.

But she did not like to think about the long-fingered hands that had held her strings.

Now that the Museum of the Peculiar Arts was closing,

Penny's time in her cabinet would soon become another memory swallowed in fog. She was certain that Fortunato was going to pack her up and put her in storage along with the rest of his collection. She didn't particularly relish the thought of eternity in a dark box, but she was a practical puppet and had long anticipated this misfortune. It wasn't as if anyone would put her in a puppet show, not now. She was too damaged. Her right hand was missing a pinkie, and her left, half a forefinger and a whole thumb. Also, her face was scratched, a small but deep gouge just above her chin.

Penny did not remember how she had sustained these injuries, but she strongly suspected that the man who had held her strings had something to do with it.

Perhaps storage wouldn't be so bad. Although, she would no longer be able to hear the radio programs Fortunato put on after hours as he swept and dusted. She found the game shows and true-crime stories particularly entertaining, and she loved *Storm at Dawn* for its sensible message of preparing for the constant threat of doomsday.

But her favorite program came on after *Storm*. It was music broadcast live from Club Heavenly Blues. When the drums would kick in, with an upbeat bass line thumping beneath the reedy saxophone and the singer's husky, beautiful voice, Penny wished she could dance.

Not because someone was pulling her strings. Just dancing, all on her own. Moving.

Penny did not know what that would be like. But music

made her think about dancing, and feeling, and emotions. Songs with fast beats and cheerful melodies made her wonder what laughing felt like. Slower songs with mournful words made her wonder about crying, the strangeness of having your sadness leak from your eyes.

If water came out of Penny's eyes, it might damage the wood. Her face would get soggy and rot. She imagined this often: warping, molding, termites eating their way out of her eye sockets.

She thought about this now as she watched Fortunato dusting the spines of his books. He looked like a weed, thin and slightly bent, as if bracing himself against a constant wind. Penny knew that he would not be selling the museum unless circumstances were dire. She figured he was probably experiencing what the Storm called "dread."

Dread, she imagined the Storm saying, the radio crackle a thin layer over his smooth voice, *that cold snake that slithers up your spine, into your chest, wrapping around your heart and squeezing.*

Penny found this to be a very dramatic, and highly entertaining, description of that emotion. The Storm was always very dramatic. Sometimes she would try to imagine how he would describe other emotions.

Excitement, that burst of bright gold fireworks that sets your whole world shimmering and sparkling.

Sadness, that thundercloud behind your eyes that casts a shadow over your soul and dampens the warmth of your heart.

Love . . .

Penny could never come up with a decent description for love. It was certainly a topic that came up in radio programs and songs frequently enough, but none explained it in a way that helped her imagine it. Then again, it was possible she wasn't imagining the others correctly either. After all, she'd never felt any of them.

Wood could not feel.

That never stopped Penny from trying, though. Just for fun. And sometimes she didn't have to try very hard.

When Fortunato's apprentice opened the door to the museum, for example, it was easy for Penny to imagine feeling happy.

THE SOUL-STEALING TYPE

Chance felt eyes on his back when he entered the museum. He paused in the doorway and looked over his shoulder.

The mostly residential street had been run-down until the war, after which more affluent citizens began taking an interest in the area. The renovated brownstone apartments were deemed "charming," and the neighborhood "booming." The squat museum had clung to its crumbling gray facade, making it somewhat of an eyesore. Two gargoyles sat sentinel on either side of the roof, their leers perhaps not as fierce as they had once been now that their teeth were chipped, their mouths gaping. But the neighborhood around the museum thrived, with gleaming glass and steel quickly replacing brick and stone.

Near the fancy hat shop at the intersection across from the park, Chance found the source of the staring. A tall, thin man in a dark gray cloak. The moment their eyes locked, the man vanished around the corner.

Chance frowned. Even from a distance, the man's face seemed odd. Smooth and sharp in an unnatural way.

Clearly a villain. Or he would be if this were an episode of *Storm at Dawn*. Villains were always lurking around wearing cloaks. They were fairly predictable.

At least in stories. Chance had never met a real-life villain.

"Fortunato?" Chance called. He let the door close behind him, bells tinkling overhead.

"Back here, my boy!" came the response.

Chance picked up speed, expertly slipping between two cabinets showcasing old coins of dubious origins, then hopping over a petrified tortoise shell. "Hi."

The man looked up from his sweeping. He was all sorts of gray, but in a nice way: charcoal eyes over a salt-and-pepper beard, hair that shone silver under the lights. He smiled back at Chance.

"I wasn't expecting any help today! Don't your parents have you busy packing?"

"We're almost finished," Chance lied. "There's a creepy-looking guy watching the museum."

Fortunato returned his attention to the dusty floor. "Is that so? How exciting."

Pushing his hair out of his eyes, Chance looked up at the marionette on the shelf behind Fortunato. "Hi, Penny."

The marionette stared back at him. Absolutely nothing about her ever changed. She was made of walnut wood, dark brown with a golden sheen, and her hair was black and curly. There was no flicker in her brown eyes, no twitch of her lips. But ever since the first time he saw her, Chance had had the strangest sensation that she was just dying to speak.

When Fortunato wasn't around, Chance talked to her. Marionettes were excellent listeners. They made good secret keepers, too.

Fortunato tossed Chance a dustrag and turned up the radio. They worked without speaking, as they always did. But Chance noticed the worry lines around Fortunato's eyes, the tightness in his smile: the expression adults wore when something was wrong but they felt the need to hide it. Chance's parents often had the same tension in their forced happy expressions. They preferred to pretend that whatever was bothering them didn't exist.

Chance and Fortunato quickly settled into their comfortable routine of dusting and sweeping. Fortunato did not pay Chance to help out around the museum, but that was fine. Chance always enjoyed examining the curious objects, no matter how many times he'd seen them. His favorite was the brown steeple hat said to have been perched atop Rip Van Winkle's head the whole two decades he had slept. Chance frequently attempted to open the great oak cabinet near Fortunato's office, but it was sealed shut. It was beautifully crafted, and the wood gleamed in a way that shouldn't have been possible, given the museum's dim lighting. Chance had heard many museum visitors speculate that this was, in fact, *the* cabinet—the one that held the chambers. And while Fortunato never confirmed these rumors, he never denied them either. After all, the idea that the chambers might still exist couldn't be bad for business.

Often Fortunato would entertain Chance with greatly exaggerated stories about his famous papa, sometimes quoting directly from the old tale *The Cabinetmaker's Apprentice*. Chance loved imagining the endless cabinets full of wonders, and when he was younger, the story of the apprentice's evil puppet had given him many a nightmare. But Chance was too old for fairy tales now. And he could never decide whether Fortunato believed his own words. It was hard to tell with a man who owned a pair of silver-plated shears he claimed had once cut off a person's shadow.

Several times Chance had nearly asked Fortunato what he planned on doing with Penny, but then he'd stopped himself. It wasn't his business, and the topic of the museum's fate clearly bothered Fortunato.

But he wondered. Because Penny was one of the last remaining lifelike, life-size marionettes from a puppet show that only the city's oldest residents remembered. Whoever had built those marionettes had been inspired by *The Cabinetmaker's Apprentice,* and rumors about them had been contorted and exaggerated until no one could separate fact from fiction. People said the marionettes weren't just lifelike. They were *alive.* Or they wanted to be.

And if given the opportunity, they would steal a child's soul for their own.

Chance glanced at Penny again. She didn't look like the soul-stealing type.

He had often wondered why Fortunato never bothered to fix her up. Replace her missing fingers, smooth out the scratch on her chin. Her black pigtails were a bit matted too. But she was otherwise an impressively realistic puppet. The kind you couldn't stop staring at. Selling her wouldn't have been enough to save the museum, but surely Fortunato could use the money.

The thought broke Chance's heart a little bit, though he'd never admit it.

"Do you want to take her?"

Startled, Chance nearly dropped the glittering meteorite he'd been dusting. Fortunato, still sweeping, nodded at Penny.

"What? I . . . no," Chance said, flustered. "Unless . . . you don't want her?"

Fortunato studied the floor, though his broom had fallen still. "I've had her for a long time, but she's yours, if you like. Consider it a thank-you and a going-away gift. Otherwise I'll put her in storage."

He looked at Chance, his gray eyebrows knit like two scrunched-up caterpillars. His mouth was smiling, but his eyes were not. In fact, Chance had the distinct impression that Fortunato wanted him to say no.

But if that meant Penny would be packed away in a box . . .

Chance nodded firmly. "Yes, please. I'd like to take her."

Fortunato closed his eyes briefly. "Good," he whispered. "Good." He nodded once, then pulled a ladder over to the cabinet. Chance watched as the museum owner climbed each rung until he stood at eye level with Penny. Carefully, he lifted her from the spot that had been her home for so long. A cloud of dust sparkled around her as Fortunato descended the ladder. Once on the floor, he hesitated before turning to Chance and holding out the puppet.

Chance swallowed. *Lifelike, life-size.* But he'd never realized just how true those words were until he stood face to face with Penny. She was indeed nearly as tall as Chance, and though he was too old to believe in such things, he couldn't help but think there was some magic involved in her design. Penny looked no more made of wood and paint than the petrified tortoise.

"See here," Fortunato said in hushed tones. He turned

Penny around, and Chance saw the strings coming from her legs and arms, all coiled and tied neatly behind her neck. "Take great care with her strings, understand? That's the secret of these marionettes, you know. Their strings." He paused, gazing at Penny, and Chance noticed his eyes were shiny. "So . . . so take care with them."

"I will," Chance promised.

Fortunato held out the marionette, and Chance took her with both hands, staggering a bit under her weight. His fingers grazed the string running from her elbow to her neck, and at once an unfamiliar but pleasant voice spoke clearly in his mind.

This probably isn't what the Storm would do, Chance.

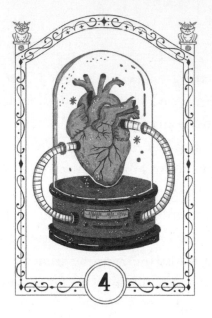

FISH FACE

Shock, that jolt of lightning that strikes you right at the core and shuts off your power.

Penny had never been this close to Chance's face. He was apparently frozen in surprise, so she now had the opportunity to notice features she hadn't before. From her seat on the top shelf, she had observed that Chance's eyes were bluish green and his hair was wavy and dark yellow, and if his skin were wood, it would be something extra-light, like birch or balsa. But she had not known about the pale freckles scattered across his cheeks, more on the right than on the left. Or the shadowy circles under his eyes.

He was gaping at her like the petrified fish on the ceiling. Penny wasn't sure why.

At last Chance said, "What?"

And Fortunato looked at him sharply. "What?"

And Penny thought, *What?*

And Chance dropped her.

His face fell away, and now Penny was staring at the ceiling, and then the floor, and then Fortunato's furrowed brows. "Careful, now," the man said over Chance's hasty apologies. But Penny didn't mind. This was the most she'd moved in ages.

Chance swung her upright again. Her toes dragged the floor. It was almost like dancing. Fortunato and Chance were still talking, but Penny wasn't paying attention. Because Chance was still holding her, and now he was saying goodbye to the museum owner and walking carefully past the shelves to the door, and Penny was about to go *outside.*

It seemed that storage was not her fate after all. At least not yet. If she were a real person, Penny imagined, she might feel excitement and gratitude.

Bells tinkled overhead, and then Penny was out of the museum. She got the briefest glimpse of the street, the tidy brownstone apartments with flowers on the windowsills, before Chase turned to face a small door just to the left of the museum entrance. He dug in his pocket with one hand, his other arm awkwardly supporting Penny. Her face was buried in his shoulder.

She sighed inwardly. *Now I can't see anything.*

"S-sorry," Chance gasped. His fingers shook as he tried to fit his key into the lock.

The door swung open to reveal a narrow staircase. Chance adjusted his hold on Penny, and now she could see again. She drank in all the details as Chance climbed the stairs. The short row of mailboxes near the door. The chipped pink paint on the walls. The creaky wooden stairs, the banister that looked as though one good pull could tear it right out of the wall. The fact that it was not the museum.

It wasn't the museum.

Penny was not in the museum anymore. Not even the Storm had ever had a greater adventure.

Now Chance stood in front of a door with the number plate 201 beneath the peephole. He twisted the doorknob, and Penny noticed that his hand was still shaking. Shaky hands meant nervousness, she remembered: the Storm often mentioned damsels in distress shaking and trembling when he encountered them. She wondered what Chance was so nervous about.

"Sorry," Chance whispered again. "It's just that I didn't know you could . . ."

He trailed off, shifting the weight of her from one arm to the other. Penny thought that if she were a person, she would probably be experiencing surprise. Because it seemed as though Chance was responding to her.

Could he *hear* her?

They passed through a short hallway with bare walls and emerged into a living room. There was a cream-colored sofa and two matching chairs, all wrapped in plastic. The floor and coffee table were covered in boxes.

Penny wished she could groan out loud. Maybe she hadn't escaped her fate after all.

"No, don't worry," Chance said, setting her down in one of the chairs. His eyes were wide; he was doing the fish face again. "I wouldn't . . . I mean, I won't let—"

"Chance?"

He jumped, backing away from the chair. Penny stared at the rest of the Bonvillain family up close for the first time. She saw Mr. Bonvillain nearly every day—or at least she had when he'd worked at the museum. He had yellow hair and light eyes and a very square jaw, and he wore a gray suit. Mrs. Bonvillain had brown hair and dark eyes and a pointy chin and nose, and she wore a dark blue dress. Constance Bonvillain looked like her mother, but with her father's eyes. She wore a pink dress with a pattern of green flowers, a matching bow holding back her curls. All three had the same balsa-wood skin.

They looked like dolls.

Penny had never noticed that before. They were just so . . . polished. Perfect. Chance always looked like a person whose body was actually lived in. Cuts and scrapes, Band-Aids, grime around his sneakers, or a tear in his clothes. Perhaps that was because Penny had only ever seen him working and cleaning in the museum, but she suspected that Chance always wore a layer of reality. The other Bonvillains were ready to be shut away in a glass case, to be looked at but never played with.

"Chance, sweetheart," said Mrs. Bonvillain, her eyes never leaving Penny, "what is that?"

Chance's back stiffened as if he were bracing himself. "One of Fortunato's marionettes. He gave her to me as a thank-you present for helping him."

His parents looked at one another, then at Chance, then back at Penny. Then they laughed.

Penny had heard lots of different types of laughs from people who visited the museum. Laughs could say all sorts of things. Trying to categorize them was a good way for a marionette to learn about emotions. The Storm was always decoding secret messages. Penny was good at decoding laughs.

She recognized what Mr. and Mrs. Bonvillain's laugh meant immediately: *"This is confusing."*

"Now, son," said Mr. Bonvillain, "it was very nice of

you to humor the poor man, but surely you don't want to keep a . . . doll."

I'm a marionette, not a doll, Penny thought at him with no small degree of indignation. There was an important difference. Dolls did not have strings.

"Yes, I do." Chance sounded nervous. "I'm keeping her."

"But why, dear?"

"Why not?" he replied. "Constance has dolls."

"Because she's a girl!" Mrs. Bonvillain exclaimed. "You don't see Constance asking for—for toy trucks or footballs."

She laughed again, and Penny decoded: *"This is still confusing."*

Mr. Bonvillain laughed too. *"This is making me uncomfortable."*

Constance giggled. *"This is funny!"* Then she stopped and tilted her head. "Wait. What's so funny about that?"

Her parents ignored her. So did Chance.

"I know none of you are going to miss Fortunato and his museum, but I am," he said loudly. "So I'm keeping Penny. And she's not a doll; she's a marionette."

With that, he picked Penny up and walked awkwardly out of the living room in a sort of two-step. Penny saw his parents clearly over his shoulder. They were deliberately looking at anything but her. She wondered if it was because of her scratched face and missing fingers.

Chance entered another room and set Penny in a chair.

This room had a bed and a desk and more boxes. She watched Chance attempt to close his door, then stumble back when Constance burst in wielding a hairbrush.

"She's so pretty!" Constance cooed, kneeling down and beaming at Penny. "Here, I just want to fix her hair up." And without waiting for permission from either her brother or his marionette, she began working the knots out of Penny's pigtails. "I can't believe Fortunato just *gave* her to you. Although she *is* a little damaged. Look at that scar on her chin! I wonder if I can fix that, maybe a little makeup. . . . Really, though, she's so realistic—just like in *The Cabinetmaker's Apprentice*. Except I'm sure she's not evil!"

If Penny could have laughed, she would have laughed scornfully, right in Constance's face. Penny had heard the old tale a hundred times over from museum patrons who pointed at her as they whispered and tittered nervously. The stupid story about the apprentice who had built demon marionettes so lifelike that all they were missing were souls. They would hypnotize children, then convince them to willingly give their own souls away so that the puppets could come alive. Because of that story, most visitors kept their distance from Penny, staring with varying expressions of amusement, curiosity, and fear.

I don't want your silly old soul, Penny would think loudly at them. *You can keep it.*

Chance hovered behind his sister throughout her

breathless stream of one-sided conversation. He looked impatient but did not attempt to interrupt her. Maybe he'd just learned that it was impossible to get a word in edgewise.

Penny focused her attention on Constance's face. Up close, her features were still doll-like and perfect. Their eyes locked, and Constance paused.

"Wow," she whispered, leaning closer. "Her eyes are so *real*. It's like she's listening to me."

"Can you leave?" Chance blurted out.

Constance looked at her brother. "Rude," she said, but she was smiling. Penny had the distinct impression this girl smiled more often than not. She wondered if Constance's mouth ever got sore.

"Sorry." Chance did not sound sorry. "It's just that I've still got packing to do." He gestured around his messy room.

"That's an understatement." Constance stood and smoothed her dress. "May I visit Penny after dinner, though?"

"Sure, I guess."

"Thank you." Constance patted Penny on the head. "Don't let her steal your soul!" she added cheerfully on her way out. Chance closed the door behind his sister with a sigh of relief, then hurried over to Penny. He held his hands out, then hesitated.

"I heard you," he said finally. "I heard your voice in my head when I touched your strings."

Interesting, thought Penny.

31

"So . . . so I want to try it again. If that's okay with you."

Penny could not give him permission, so she just watched as Chance reached out and touched the string running from her wrist up the back of her arm. He looked nervous, and she wished she could smile.

Hi, Fish Face, she thought, and if she could have laughed at his expression, she would have.

A BOY PUPPET

Chance's mouth opened and closed several times. "H-hello," he finally managed to stammer. "Um . . ."

He didn't know what to say. But he wanted to hear her voice again.

Actually, *hear* wasn't the right word. He wanted to *feel* her voice again. It was soft and pleasant and resonated inside his head in a curious way, like the hammers gently tapping the strings inside a piano.

I didn't know you'd be able to hear me, Penny said. *This is strange.*

"It is," Chance agreed. "I wonder why Fortunato never mentioned this?"

He never heard me, Penny told him. *At least he never responded like you did.*

"Did he ever touch your strings?" Chance asked. "Because that's the only way I can hear you."

He probably did at some point. He hasn't taken me out of my cabinet for as long as I can remember, though.

Her tone was very matter-of-fact, but Chance suddenly felt deeply sorry for her. How horrible, he thought, to be stuck up on a shelf for so long that you couldn't recall anything else.

Your family is moving, Penny said. *Does that mean you have to pack me in a box?*

"No! I promise I won't," Chance assured her. "Besides, I'm not . . ." He paused, glancing at his closed door again, and lowered his voice. "I'm not going with them. I'm running away."

That sounds exciting! Where will you go?

Chance had not discussed his plans with anyone yet, and now the words tumbled out. "There's a carnival that sets up in the park every summer. They're leaving in a few weeks to travel around the country. I'm going to see if I can get a job with them, help run one of the games or take tickets or—or even clean up horse poop. Anything! I just . . . I can't move to Daystar Meadows, because . . ."

34

He stopped, because this part was harder to put into words. After a moment, Penny finished his thought.

Because your parents didn't even ask if it was okay with you, because they were happy about the museum closing and didn't care that you were upset, because all the things they hate about the museum and the city are all the stuff you love most, and because you're tired of the way they want life to be perfect and safe and boring?

Chance gaped at her again. "Well . . . yeah. How did you know that?"

You told me. You always talk to me when Fortunato isn't around.

Of course he had. Chance felt incredibly embarrassed about all his confessions now that he knew Penny really *had* been listening. A flush crept up his neck as he tried to remember everything else he'd said while doing chores around the museum.

Is your sister running away too?

Chance snorted. "No way. She's excited about the move. And she'd never do that to my parents. I'm going to write her letters, though," he added hastily. "I don't want any of them to worry about me. I mean, I know they will, no matter what. But I'll let them know I'm okay."

Saying it out loud made him uncomfortable. In his mind, Chance had assured himself he had nothing to feel guilty about. He loved his family, and he wasn't running away to hurt them. But he did not fit in. He wanted adventure and excitement and, yes, maybe a little bit of danger. Everything the other Bonvillains did their best to avoid.

It wasn't that he never wanted to see them again. But it was all too much: a new house, a new school, leaving the city and the museum behind. . . . If he moved to Daystar Meadows, there would be no break from the monotony.

Penny's voice interrupted his thoughts. *Constance seemed to like me. Do you think she'd want to keep me while you're gone?*

"What?" Chance blinked. "No, you're coming with me!"

Really?

In retrospect, he wasn't sure when he'd decided this. Probably the moment Fortunato had offered to give Penny to him. Leaving her behind had never been an option.

"Yes," he said firmly. "Maybe . . . maybe we could even put together an act or something! There's always magicians and clowns and ventriloquists at the carnival."

That would be wonderful! Penny's voice was instantly brighter. *Do you think you could be a puppeteer?*

Chance shrugged. "Let's find out."

With great care, he untied the delicate knot of strings at the base of her neck. There were eight in total: one for each knee, hand, and shoulder, one on her back, and one coming from the top of her head. The strings glimmered strangely; they were wispy, yet Chance felt certain he could not break one even if he wanted to. Each string was seamlessly connected to Penny, as if it had been drawn directly out of the wood.

We're almost the same height, Penny pointed out. *You'll have to stand on something.*

"Oh, right!" Chance straightened up and hurried over to his desk. He dragged the chair to the center of his room. Then he returned to Penny and, very carefully, picked her up and sat her on the floor in front of the chair. He took the strings connected to her head and right limbs in his right hand, and the strings connected to her back and left limbs in his left hand. Slowly he stepped onto the chair. Then he lifted Penny off the ground.

I'm standing! Oh, I can see us in the mirror.

Chance lifted his left hand experimentally. The whole of the left side of Penny's body rose awkwardly in response, and he couldn't help laughing. "Sorry. It'd be a lot easier with one of those wooden controller things most puppets have. Maybe I can ask Fortunato to make one."

That might help. You're very bad at this.

"Hey," Chance said, but he was still smiling. He continued raising and lowering his hands, quickly realizing that smaller movements were easier to control. After a few minutes, he was able to move only her legs and then only her arms. A flick of his right hand and she bowed. Tilting both hands inward resulted in her waving both arms; tilting them outward caused her to kick both legs.

I'm starting to look a little less ridiculous, Penny mused. *Do you really think we can get a job at the carnival?*

Chance nodded eagerly. "I really do. And the move isn't for another week, so—oops, sorry." He winced, snatching up the string that had slipped from his hand. Penny's left leg flailed wildly.

Only a week? We've got a lot of practicing to do.

And so they did.

On Monday, Chance figured out how to make Penny walk without her arms swinging in tandem with her legs. He packed all the books on his shelf into a box his mother gave him, sneaking his favorite comics into the runaway backpack he kept under his bed. When he realized Penny had never read a comic, he propped one up in front of her to read as he packed, and turned the page for her every few minutes.

On Tuesday, due to an overambitious attempt at a pirouette, Chance spent most of the morning untangling Penny's strings while they debated whether clairvoyance was a better superpower than telepathy. The discussion was cut short when Constance arrived with her sewing kit and insisted on patching up the moth holes in Penny's dress. (She informed Chance that invisibility was the best power. Chance and Penny later agreed that Constance had a lot to learn about superheroes.)

On Wednesday, Penny managed a decent jig before kicking Chance so hard it left a purple bruise on his shin.

She read more comics while Chance packed up his board games and action figures. That night he fell asleep still holding Penny's strings as she described what little memories of performing she had, and his dreams were filled with fog.

On Thursday they managed three successful pirouettes in a row. Chance hugged Penny and spun her around the room in his excitement, and then, deeply embarrassed by his actions, he spent the rest of the afternoon cleaning out his closet.

On Friday they had a breakthrough.

Chance stood on the chair, eyes closed, hands gripping the strings. He was attempting to make Penny execute a brief bit of choreography he remembered from his sister's ballet recital last spring. His concentration was so intense he barely noticed the strange feeling creeping under his skin, like veneer coating his insides. Penny stayed silent as he worked. Until:

Chance. Look at us.

With great effort, Chance opened his eyes. He stared at their reflection. Penny was frozen in a graceful pose, her mangled hands poised delicately over her head, her left leg bent at the knee, toes touching her right calf. Her face glowed, her dark eyes alight with happiness. Above her hovered a boy puppet, his eyes glassy, his arms stiff.

Not a boy puppet. Chance.

The shock took a few seconds too long to hit. Then Chance gasped for air as if he'd just resurfaced after far too long underwater. He jerked his hands free of the strings, and Penny hit the floor in a clatter of wooden arms and legs.

"I'm sorry!" Chance cried in horror as he jumped off the chair. Gently he sat Penny up and touched the string at her wrist. "Are you okay?"

I'm fine, she told him. *How did you do that?*

"I don't know," Chance said truthfully. He still felt odd, as if he'd just woken abruptly from a deep sleep. "I was imagining doing the move myself. But . . . but as you."

You imagined you were me?

"Sort of, yes," he replied, wishing he could explain it better. "I don't know. It was almost like . . . like I was under a spell."

Ah. Penny's tone had changed to something more guarded. *Well, I wasn't trying to cast a spell on you. I'm not a soul thief.*

"I know!" Chance said hurriedly. "That's not what I meant. I just felt . . . weird."

He couldn't help glancing at his reflection again. His eyes were wide, and he was a little paler than usual. But he looked *real,* much to his relief.

"Chance?" Mrs. Bonvillain's voice interrupted the awkward moment. Chance dropped the string and turned around, blocking his mother's view of Penny. "Can you run to the hardware store? We're almost out of packing tape."

"Okay!" Chance waited until Mrs. Bonvillain had left

before touching Penny's string again. "I'll be right back, all right?"

All right.

Chance hesitated because he felt like he should say something else. Reassure Penny that he knew she wasn't a soul thief, that she would never do such a terrible thing. But the image of what they had looked like in the mirror was vivid in his mind, and the memory of his own glassy eyes reflected back at him caused his stomach to turn. So he just nodded, let go of her string, and left his room.

The moment he closed his door, the man who'd been crouched on the fire escape stood to his full height, quietly opened the window, and slipped inside like a shadow.

NOTHING

Penny heard the soft padding of footsteps behind her. A moment later, a man knelt down and looked her in the eyes.

She had seen him before, many times. He had visited Fortunato frequently in the last few weeks, and his oddly sharp face was memorable. Penny had thought perhaps he was the man who was buying the museum.

But seeing as he had just broken into Chance's room, he clearly had intentions much more sinister than purchasing real estate.

"You don't remember me," the man murmured, "do you."

It was not a question. Penny watched him curiously, because she sensed he was referring not to his museum visits but to something further back. And the sound of his voice had dislodged a memory that had been trapped long ago by the fog. . . . Penny couldn't quite grasp an image, but she could hear cheers and whistles.

The man with the sharp face reached for her head. He was going to steal her, Penny was certain. But instead, he pulled up the string connected to her head and held it taut.

With his other hand, he took a pair of scissors from within his cloak. Smiling coldly, he whispered:

"This won't hurt a bit."

Snip.

The man, the boxes, Chance's bed and dresser . . . everything vanished, and Penny fell through dense, impenetrable fog. Seconds passed like centuries. The world was muted and colorless and endless. Penny was nothing, floating in nothing.

It was fine, she told herself. Memories of Chance and dancing and the idea of a carnival life were fading fast, disappearing in the gray. And it wouldn't have mattered even if they had run away together. In the end, this was Penny's fate, the fate of all marionettes.

The worst had finally happened. But that was fine. She had prepared herself for this.

It was a very good thing, Penny thought vaguely, that wood could not feel the pain of loss, because hers would be too overwhelming to endure.

A MYSTERIOUS PACKAGE FROM AN ENEMY

Glue wouldn't hold. Tape wouldn't stick. The stapler seemed too cruel.

Chance had done everything he could to reattach Penny's string. But it was impossible. He'd even snuck his mother's sewing kit into his room and threaded the string on a needle, intending to sew it right into Penny's scalp. But sewing, as it turned out, did not work on wood.

Penny's voice was gone. When Chance touched her other strings, there was no response, nothing. He'd thought she was ignoring him, until he spotted the loose string

spread neatly across her lap. It was as if someone had plucked it out and left it there for Chance to find.

But who, *who* would do such a thing? And why just one string? And how had it been done so quickly? Chance had been gone for only ten minutes at most, and his mother and sister had been home the whole time. His first thought was that perhaps Constance had come in to brush Penny's hair, but she had been in her room, still wrapping her delicate figurines in newspaper, when Chance returned. And besides, if Constance had accidentally pulled Penny's string out, she would have told Chance. She was honest that way.

Chance fretted silently all through dinner and his bath. Fortunately, his parents were too distracted with the move to notice any difference in his behavior. He climbed into bed and stared at Penny and wondered if this meant she was dead.

Well after midnight, Chance drifted off into an uneasy sleep, the loose string still clutched in his fingers.

He awoke late the next morning to find his mother packing Penny into a box.

"Stop!" Chance leaped out of bed and grabbed Mrs. Bonvillain's arm. His brain felt covered with cobwebs. "Don't pack her! I . . . um, there'll be room in the car. I'll take her on the drive."

His mother's lips twisted in a funny, tight smile. "Now, Chance," she said, "it's safer for it to be in a box. The car is going to be full. What if it gets damaged?" Her eyes flickered from Penny's mangled hands to her scarred face. "Er, damaged further?"

"I'll put her on my lap."

Mrs. Bonvillain's smile hardened even more. "Like Constance did with her dollies when she was little?"

Chance did not move, but he dropped his gaze to the floor. He didn't like the way his mother was looking at him. As if she were waiting for him to realize he had something to be ashamed of.

Which he did. But it certainly wasn't trying to keep Penny safe. It was the fact that he'd allowed her to break in the first place.

"Chance."

His mother knelt down in front of him. Chance blinked in surprise and dropped his arms.

"I know what this is about," Mrs. Bonvillain said softly. "Moving is hard. But believe me, it's for the best. You're going to *love* Daystar Meadows. We'll have a backyard! And your new bedroom is twice the size of this one!"

Chance chewed his lip. He didn't care about backyards or bigger bedrooms, and he wasn't going to Daystar Meadows. But now that the fuzzy feeling in his head was subsiding, the reality of his situation was beginning to dawn. His family was moving tomorrow, and he had to find Fortunato and get him to fix Penny before then. Chance couldn't go to the carnival without her. In just one short week, they'd become friends. And though he hated

47

to admit it, the idea of running away to the carnival was a bit more intimidating now that the time for action had nearly arrived. He wanted to be brave, but he needed Penny with him.

His mother was still waiting for a response. Before Chance could open his mouth, his stomach growled loudly.

"How about we get you some lunch, sleepyhead," Mrs. Bonvillain said, ruffling his hair, "and we'll figure out what can fit in the car afterward?"

"Okay."

Chance followed her out of his room, squeezing the loose string in his hand. When he passed the front door, he heard a muffled click. "Mom, I think the mail's here," he said dully.

"Can you get that for me, dear?"

"Sure."

He grabbed his keys off the hook, then opened the door. There, at the bottom of the stairs, was the man who had been lurking near the museum earlier that week. The man with the sharp face.

They locked eyes for a moment. Then the man took off.

"Wait!" Chance ran down the stairs, tripping in his haste. He jumped the last three steps and burst outside, looking up and down the street frantically. But the man with the sharp face was gone.

Heart pounding in his ears, Chance peered around more carefully. How could the man have vanished so quickly?

More importantly, why had he been in the entrance to Chance's apartment? And who *was* he?

Chance allowed the door to swing shut as he stepped over to the mailboxes on the wall. He unlocked the Bonvillains' mailbox, pondering the man's face. It was all angles, but in the most peculiar way. He looked as if he'd been drawn by Mrs. Bonvillain's favorite painter, whose subjects always came out looking jagged and abstract. His cheeks were hollowed out, his chin a sharp point, his nose so short it almost looked like a regular-size nose that had been shaved down to a squarish nub.

It was a moment before Chance noticed the bright yellow envelope among all the bills. For a few seconds, Chance forgot all about the man with the sharp face. He raced up the stairs, tossed the other mail onto the coffee table, and sprinted to his room.

Constance was there, fussing over Penny's hair again.

"Hey!" Chance cried. "You can't just come into my room without knocking."

"I did knock," Constance told him. "You weren't here."

While his sister continued playing with Penny's hair, Chance headed over to his dresser with the yellow envelope. At the end of every episode of *Storm at Dawn*, there was a message to decode. Listeners could then send their translations in to the show by postcard, and if they were correct, they would receive a prize. This was the sixth prize Chance had won. Most of them had been somewhat disappointing: cheap plastic whistles and rings. But Chance still sent in for them.

He turned the envelope over and blinked. The Storm's wax seal, which bore the mark of an eye narrowed in suspicion, was loose.

Someone had opened his prize already.

Is that what the man with the sharp face had been doing downstairs? But how would he have opened the mailbox without a key? In fact—Chance berated himself for not considering this sooner—how had the man unlocked the entrance to the stairwell? Only the Bonvillains and Fortunato had keys.

Taking a deep breath, Chance set the envelope down. This was what he'd wanted, wasn't it? A mystery, an adventure complete with a villain. And a quest: his quest to fix Penny. An opportunity to be a hero. So how would the Storm handle this?

First and foremost, the Storm would exercise great caution when dealing with a mysterious package from an enemy. Chance glanced in the mirror to make sure Constance was still preoccupied with Penny. Then he grabbed two tissues to protect his hands. Carefully he picked up the envelope and turned it over. Something fell onto his dresser with a solid *thunk*.

Chance leaned down to examine the odd object. This was not made of the same cheap plastic as his other toys from the Storm. It was an ornately carved disk roughly the size of Chance's palm, made of whitish wood polished to such a shine that he couldn't see the grain. Attached to the disk was a long, thick needle made of silver so light it almost appeared translucent. It looked very old-fashioned, but it also reminded Chance of the big blue sewing machine they'd gotten his mother for her last birthday. That machine had a similar piece on top. His mother would wrap thread around the thick needle to keep it from getting tangled, and the disk would feed the thread into the machine.

Two thoughts popped into Chance's head at the same time.

First, the man with the sharp face had stolen his prize and replaced it with this thing.

Second, Chance could use it to fix Penny.

Was that what the man with the sharp face wanted him to do? For that matter, how would he have known Chance had Penny in the first place?

Chance pictured him lurking outside the museum on Sunday and frowned. He could have been watching when Chance carried Penny into his apartment.

But how could he possibly have known Penny was broken? Unless he was the one who had broken her . . .

The Storm would never trust such a stranger who snuck and lurked. But Chance found himself entranced by the strange object. Besides, he was desperate.

"Lunch is ready!" Mrs. Bonvillain called from the

kitchen. Quickly Chance scooped up the object and turned around, keeping his hands behind his back.

"Be right there!" he called.

Constance stood and patted Penny on the head. "Doesn't her hair look better now?" She pointed at the long, thick braid hanging down Penny's back, curls pinned down with numerous bobby pins.

"Sure," Chance said, and Constance looked pleased.

She headed to the door, then turned around. "Aren't you coming?"

Chance squeezed the object in his right hand. "In a minute."

"Okay." Constance tilted her head, looking from him to Penny, then back again. "Is everything okay, Chance?"

"What? Yes! Why?"

His sister shrugged. "It's just that you've been acting kind of weird about Penny. And, well . . . you remember what happened in *The Cabinetmaker's Apprentice*, right? That marionette the apprentice built cast a spell on him and—"

Chance shifted uncomfortably. "That's just a stupid story, Constance. It's not real."

His sister pressed her lips together. "You're right," she said after a moment. "I'm just being silly." But he noticed the way her eyes flickered one last time over to Penny before she closed the door.

Chance didn't waste a second. First, he took a small needle from his mother's sewing kit, threaded Penny's string through the eye, and knotted it carefully. Then he wound the length of string around the longer needle attached to the disk. The string wasn't very long, and it struck Chance that this was both an unnecessary and an entirely unhelpful step. He'd already tried sewing, after all, and couldn't even make a dent in Penny's wooden head.

But this object had an odd sheen that, as ridiculous as it sounded, made it like something from a fairy tale. An ordinary object with extraordinary magic. And Chance was willing to try anything.

He knelt down at Penny's side and gently prodded her scalp with the sewing needle. It sank right through her scalp.

"Sorry!" Chance cried, although he wasn't sure if she could even feel it, much less hear him. His heart raced, the strange object spinning in his hand as he tugged the needle and string through.

Hang on, Penny, he thought, *I'm coming for you,* and that thought made no sense at all. And yet it did, because now Chance felt like he was descending, climbing down a rope into endless fog. The object shimmered and spun in his hand, and his hand shimmered too; his skin was practically glowing, and this was magic—Chance knew it for sure now—and it was going to work. He concentrated so hard his vision blurred as he sank deeper and deeper into the abyss.

He pulled and pulled the string, and it took much longer than it should have for him to realize that the string had not been this long before; it had been only an arm's length, but somehow now there was so much of it, and the object wasn't spinning in his hand anymore—the whole room was spinning around it; in fact, the whole world was spinning, as if the object were the sun around which the entire galaxy revolved and Chance were a star with light spilling out of all five points, and the last thought he had before blackness swallowed him was *This string isn't string at all.*

A SPINDLE FROM A
SPINNING WHEEL

Penny opened her eyes.

Then she closed them.

Then she opened them.

She experimented with blinking. She appeared to be facedown on the carpet, which was beige and patterned like diamonds.

It disappeared when she blinked. Beige diamonds. Black. Beige diamonds. Black.

The carpet was scratchy. She could feel it on her skin, because she had skin now instead of wood. Her arms and face itched, and the sensation was delightful. Instinct kicked in, and Penny scratched her cheek with her right hand. Then a jolt of excitement ripped through her.

She could *move.*

Penny shot to her feet, swayed, and fell back onto the carpet. She laughed and heard her voice out loud. It sounded familiar, but nothing like the voice in her head. Chance's bedroom spun around her, and she closed her eyes, waiting for the sensation to fade. But she couldn't seem to stop moving. She wiggled her toes, knocked her knees together, rubbed the carpet with her fingers. She sneezed, and then she laughed again, because sneezes felt even more ridiculous than they sounded. Her right hand grazed some sort of fabric, and Penny clenched it tightly. When she opened her eyes, she saw she was holding on to her skirt.

But she was not wearing it.

A marionette was wearing it.

Penny decided that the mind fog must have driven her mad at last. Because she was looking at herself, and it wasn't a reflection. A marionette with curly black hair and dark eyes and walnut wood was slumped over next to her, wearing a pale yellow dress with a low-fitted sash. The only difference was that when Penny had seen herself in the mirror, her hair had been in pigtails. Now it was in a braid.

Stretching out her arms, Penny studied her hands. This skin was white and freckled. This body was wearing rumpled pajamas. When she ran her fingers through her hair, she found it to be short and fine and wavy.

"I don't understand," Penny said out loud, and now she knew why her voice didn't sound the same as it did in her head. Because it wasn't her voice at all.

Slowly Penny stood and faced herself in the mirror. Chance's reflection stared back at her.

"Well," said Penny. "This is interesting."

She flexed her arms and bounced up and down on her toes—*his* toes, technically. Moving was more wonderful than she'd imagined, muscles and bones and joints all responding to her brain's commands instantly. Widening her eyes, she smiled as broadly as she could and watched Chance's lips stretch. Then she felt an unpleasant, constricting feeling in her gut.

Worry, those tiny termites gnawing their way out of your stomach.

Kneeling down, Penny sat the marionette upright and leaned it against the chair. The string had been reattached to its head somehow. She touched it, and Chance's voice filled her head.

What happened? Why can't I move?

"Oh," said Penny. "Oh dear."

He was trapped inside the marionette.

Penny?

Yes, Penny thought, then shook her head. "Yes," she told him out loud. "I'm in your body. I don't know how it happened."

I did it by accident. The pitch of his voice was higher than normal. Panic, Penny realized. That was what happened on *Storm at Dawn* when a character panicked. High voice, irrational decisions.

"Don't worry," she said. "I'll switch us back. Just tell me how you did it."

Do you see a wooden disk? There's a huge needle attached to it.

Penny glanced around the carpet. Something silver glinted from under the chair, and she retrieved the object. "Here it is." Studying the disk and needle more closely, Penny felt yet another new emotion, but it was one she couldn't name. Was there a word for sensing familiarity in something you'd never seen before?

"I know what this is," she heard herself say. "It's a spindle from a spinning wheel." Kneeling, she touched the marionette's string again. "Where did you get it?"

There was a pause. And then Chance's thoughts spilled out so fast Penny could barely keep up. She listened closely to every word.

"The man with the sharp face came in through the window," Penny informed him when he'd finished. "He cut the string off my head with scissors."

Chance groaned. *I shouldn't have used that thing. I should have known better. The Storm would have never . . .*

Penny turned the spindle over in her hand. It looked as though it belonged on a shelf of oddities.

"Well, it worked," Penny pointed out, hoping to make Chance feel better. "The string is back in place. Us swapping like this is just a . . . side effect."

In the pause that followed, Penny could sense Chance's confusion.

"What?" she prompted.

It's just . . . you think we swapped? Swapped what?

"Bodies," Penny said. She thought that was perfectly obvious.

Yes, but . . . that story about the apprentice's marionette . . .

Penny sighed. "That story is nonsense. I would never steal your soul. And I don't know how to cast spells. Besides, you're the one who used the spindle in the first place, not me."

Oh. That's true.

"And," Penny continued rather defensively, "if I'd stolen your soul, I would have come alive, like in the story. But the marionette is still just a marionette." She nudged its motionless wooden leg for emphasis.

That's a good point.

"Thank you." Penny held up the spindle and examined it. "Now. What did you do with this, exactly?"

I wound the loose string around the disk thing—er, spindle—and used a needle to sew the string back onto your head, and . . . Another pause followed, filled with that mixed-up, jumbly sensation. *I don't know why, but suddenly it was like your head wasn't made of wood anymore. It was soft. The needle didn't work until I used the spindle, too, and then the needle went right in, and I pulled the string through, and then I kept pulling and I got dizzy, and right before I blacked out, I realized something.*

"What?"

I . . . I don't remember.

"Hmm. So the spindle has some sort of magic?"

Yeah, it must.

Penny thought quickly. Because she had spent her whole life doing nothing but thinking, she was able to do so at an exceptionally fast speed. "I have an idea," she told Chance when she had finished. "We don't know who the man with the sharp face is, but Fortunato does, and—"

He does?!

"Yes, that man has visited the museum a lot in the last few weeks," Penny said. "My point is that Fortunato might know what he wants. In fact, he might even be able to help us swap back."

That's a good idea.

"Thank you."

Can we go right now? Chance's voice was kind of high again. *We don't have much time. My family is moving tomorrow morning, and we have to—*

A voice from the doorway startled them both.

"Chance." Mrs. Bonvillain's face was scrunched up in a strange way. She gazed at Penny the way some museum visitors gazed at the mechanical heart at the museum, with a mix of amusement and perplexity, as if they weren't exactly sure what to make of the thing. "I've been calling you for five minutes to come to lunch." Her brow furrowed even more. "Why are you holding the doll's hand?"

Penny glanced down at her hand, which was grasping the marionette's wrist. Again she thought quickly. The truthful response was *Because we swapped bodies, and the only way for me to talk to your son is by touching one of these strings.* But she felt sure Mrs. Bonvillain would not appreciate that answer. Penny had to lie about why Chance was currently holding hands with the marionette. She pictured the many couples she'd seen come and go at the museum, fingers interlaced as they examined the artifacts.

"Because we're friends," she told Mrs. Bonvillain. "Because we love each other."

Penny was proud of having thought of a perfectly plausible lie so quickly. But now Mrs. Bonvillain's expression had contorted into one far more complicated. Penny was so busy trying to decode it, several seconds passed before she realized Chance was yelling in her head.

LET GO! LET GO! LET GO!

"Oh." Penny dropped the marionette's hand, and Chance's voice vanished abruptly. "Sorry. I was . . . joking."

Mrs. Bonvillain's expression cleared somewhat. "Oh. Very funny," she said with a laugh that made it clear she did not find this in the least bit amusing. "Hurry up and eat your lunch now. We have work to do."

"Okay." Penny cast one last glance at the marionette before following Mrs. Bonvillain out of the room. She would just have to take Chance down to Fortunato after lunch.

Besides, she was looking forward to eating food for the first time.

A HERO

Chance had experienced helplessness before. Or so he'd thought. There was the time the Bonvillains' dog, Pepper, had gotten very sick, and the veterinarian had said there was nothing he could do. There was the time a burglar had broken into several homes in the neighborhood, and Chance had become highly aware of how easy it would be for someone to climb the fire escape and smash a brick through his bedroom window.

But being trapped inside a marionette was a new level of helplessness.

It wasn't just that Chance couldn't move. He couldn't talk. He couldn't feel. He was nothing but consciousness stuck inside a shell shaped like a girl. For as long as he could remember, he'd wanted action and adventure and mystery. He'd wanted to be a hero, like the Storm. This was an adventure, certainly. But it wasn't at all the kind he'd wanted.

All he could do was think and wait. That was it.

In Fortunato's apartment below him, the man with the sharp face was thinking and waiting too.

MOPPING

Penny's first meal was a peanut butter and banana sandwich. It was salty and sweet and made her tongue stick to the roof of her mouth. She did her best to control Chance's facial expressions so that his sister and mother wouldn't notice her shock at the texture of the peanut butter or her utter delight at the sweetness of the banana. Mrs. Bonvillain was too distracted with packing up the last of the dishes, but Constance watched Penny with a polite but curious smile.

The moment they'd swallowed the last bites of their sandwiches, Mrs. Bonvillain whisked Penny and Constance to the study, and the three spent nearly two hours packing books and knickknacks into boxes. After that she set them to work dusting and sweeping and mopping. Thankfully, Penny had some idea of how to do these chores, after countless evenings spent watching Fortunato and Chance clean the museum. She took great pleasure in each movement, swinging the broom around like a dance partner when no one was looking, twirling the mop and letting the soapy water spray her legs. Several times she thought of Chance trapped and unable to move in his room, and her delight was momentarily overtaken by another feeling.

Guilt, that rock that sinks from your chest down into your gut and expands into an immovable boulder.

Logically, Penny knew that she could not take Chance to Fortunato now without raising his mother's suspicion. But if she was honest with herself—which she always was—she wasn't ready to give up having a real body just yet.

The day passed into evening this way, with Penny alternating between joy and guilt. Dinner was spaghetti with tomato sauce, which Penny liked well enough, and steamed broccoli, which she found highly unpleasant in both flavor and texture. She wondered why anyone ever ate anything other than peanut butter and banana sandwiches.

Once the last dishes were cleaned and boxed, Mrs. Bonvillain filled a tub with hot water and ordered Penny to take a bath. From her stern tone, Penny sensed that Chance was often reluctant to do this, so she put up a halfhearted fuss before acquiescing, so as not to arouse suspicion. But bathing turned out to be, frankly, the most fascinating experience of her entire life. She could not imagine how anyone could detest it.

(She also figured out how to use a toilet, which was not as enjoyable as a bathtub but, as it turned out, very necessary.)

The whole day, Penny experienced flutters of that one emotion she couldn't name. The sense of familiarity. Marionettes did not bathe or wash dishes or sweep, but Penny had adapted to each activity as if she'd done them hundreds of times. Perhaps it was just Chance's body operating on instinct.

When she entered Chance's room, a new emotion jolted through Penny. She knew the word for this one because she could tell immediately that this was what Chance had felt when he'd heard her voice for the first time.

Shock.

"Where is he?"

She hurried into the room, looking behind boxes and under Chance's bed. But the marionette was gone.

Chance was gone.

Penny marched into the hallway. "Mrs. . . . ," she bellowed, then caught herself. "Mom? Where's Penny?"

From the living room, she heard Mrs. Bonvillain sigh in an exaggerated way. "I packed your doll, sweetheart. Like we discussed."

"But—"

"Chance." His mother appeared at the end of the hall, arms crossed. "It's all boxed up. You'll be able to unpack tomorrow when we get to the new house."

"But I—"

Mrs. Bonvillain held up a hand, and Penny closed her mouth. "Go to bed, dear. We've got an early morning, and a busy day ahead."

And with that, she steered Penny back into Chance's room and pointed to his bed. Penny lay down stiffly and stared at the ceiling. Mrs. Bonvillain pulled the sheets up to Penny's neck, kissed her on the forehead, and left the room, turning the lights off behind her.

Penny listened as the footsteps faded. Her eyelids were already beginning to droop, and she realized she was experiencing sleepiness. But there was no time for sleep now, not with Chance packed up in a box. Fortunately, puppets never slept, and Penny was able to fight off unconsciousness as she waited until the apartment was completely still and silent.

She threw the sheets off and leaped to her feet. "Chance?" she whispered. "Don't worry, I'm coming." Quietly Penny opened the box by the dresser and found stacks of shirts and pants. The next two boxes were filled with books. The fourth seemed to be filled with nothing but winter coats and jackets, and Penny would have closed it back up had she not seen a familiar black shoe sticking out beneath a coat sleeve.

"There you are!" She grabbed the marionette's ankle and yanked it out. Chance's voice spoke in her mind as soon as her fingers touched the string attached to the leg.

How long have I been in here?

"All day," Penny told him. "I'm very sorry. Your mother made me mop, and I didn't know she'd packed you up. Are you okay?"

Yeah, said Chance. *It was scary at first, but then I remembered the episode where the Storm gets locked in a coffin. Did you hear that one?*

"Yes!" Penny exclaimed. "He woke up and realized Madam M had drugged him and was going to bury him alive, so he went into a meditative trance."

Exactly. He said the biggest danger was running out of air, and when you panic, you start breathing heavily. Meditating helped him control his breaths.

"But marionettes don't breathe," Penny said. "It wouldn't matter if you ran out of air."

I know, Chance agreed. *I figured that out while I was meditating, and it helped me not to panic. Actually, after a while it was kind of nice.*

"It was?"

Yeah. It was peaceful. Besides, it was better than mopping, he added, and Penny could hear the smile in his voice. She smiled too.

"I liked mopping," she said. "It's wonderful being able to move around. Baths are nice too."

You took a bath?! He sounded horrified.

"Don't worry, I pretended I didn't want to," Penny reassured him. "Your mother doesn't suspect anything."

That's not what I . . . Wait, really? She can't tell at all?

"Well, she's really distracted with all the moving." Penny frowned, because even though Chance didn't respond, she felt his fear. "I'm not going to keep your body," she told him firmly. "I'm not a demon or a thief. I told you—that story about the apprentice is made-up nonsense."

I know. I trust you.

She could tell he wanted to mean it.

"Everyone's asleep now," Penny said. "Are you ready to have Fortunato switch us back?"

Are you?

At this, Penny faltered. Because in truth, she was not ready at all. She should have been grateful to have had a whole day in a real body. But she wanted more.

This wasn't her body, though. She had to do the right thing. Penny grabbed the spindle, then lifted the marionette and looked him in the eyes.

"I'm ready," she told him firmly, and carried him out of the room.

THE PUPPETEER

Chance had not been entirely honest with Penny.

It was true that he had tried using the Storm's meditation technique to calm himself during those first few minutes in the box. But realizing that marionettes didn't need air had not made him feel better. If anything, it had made him feel even more suffocated. Because breathing was the most basic form of movement he could imagine, something he'd done every moment of every day without thinking. And now he couldn't even do that.

He recalled watching his mother open the box of coats

and pull a few out, and he'd known what she was about to do. When she'd reached for him, Chance had had only a few frantic seconds to decide whether or not to speak to her. But it had turned out not to matter. Mrs. Bonvillain had taken the marionette by the braid, nose wrinkled as if she were taking out the garbage, and tossed it into the box. She had not touched the strings.

Chance had never felt so helpless in his life. Or so terrified. But he couldn't tell Penny, because . . . well, this was the reality of her entire existence. And he couldn't even handle a few hours like this? Shame mingled with his fear.

Penny was the one who had to descend back into that fog and cage herself forever, just so he could be free. Chance wouldn't blame Penny if she never wanted to swap back. That thought did little to ease his anxiety.

Now he stared over her shoulder as she crept down the hall to the front door. *Don't forget my keys,* Chance told her. *We'll be locked out.*

"Where are they?" she whispered.

Hanging on the wall to the left of the door. Mine's the one with the blue key ring.

Chance heard a muffled jingle. "Got them," Penny said. She slipped quietly out to the stairwell, and Chance watched his front door get smaller and smaller as they descended the steps.

On the second-floor landing, Penny knocked on

Fortunato's door. They waited in a hushed silence for several long seconds. She knocked again.

"It's not that late," Penny said suddenly. "He's probably still down in the museum."

She carried Chance down the last flight of stairs. He glimpsed his family's mailbox in the foyer and wondered for the millionth time about the man with the sharp face. How did he know Fortunato? More importantly, did Fortunato realize the man was a villain?

Penny shifted the weight of the marionette as she pushed through the door and stepped onto the street. "He might not be able to hear me knock over the radio. *Live from Club Heavenly Blues* might still be on. Do you ever listen to that? I—"

She stopped abruptly in front of the museum's entrance. Chance, who was still gazing out at the street over her shoulder, desperately wished he could turn around. *What's wrong?*

"It's open," Penny whispered. "Fortunato never leaves the door open."

Is he in there?

"I don't know." She fell silent for a few seconds. "I don't hear anything. No radio."

Maybe he finished cleaning early.

"And left the door unlocked?" Penny shook her head. "Something's obviously wrong. We'll have to be careful."

Easy for you to say, Chance thought. *I can't exactly do*

anything if something happens. He tried not to sound too bitter.

"Then I'll be careful enough for both of us."

Penny opened the door so slowly that the bells overhead didn't even jangle. Instinctively, Chance wanted to inhale the familiar, musty museum smell, but he was reminded once again that he could not breathe at all. He watched shelves pass as Penny tiptoed down the narrow aisles toward the back. He had never heard the museum this quiet and felt a wave of foreboding.

"I know," Penny whispered, apparently in response. "In *Storm at Dawn,* this would be the suspenseful part when you realize that Madam M is lurking in the shadows but the Storm hasn't noticed her yet."

Do you think anyone's in here?

Penny shrugged, and the marionette's head moved up and down with the gesture. "Maybe. But the worst has happened, hasn't it? We're swapped."

Things could be worse.

"How?"

I don't know. But they could always be worse.

"That's true—oh!" Penny stopped abruptly. "Fortunato's office."

Is he in there?

"It doesn't look like it," she replied. "It's all locked up. But I bet I can get in."

Penny set Chance and the spindle on top of a short glass

case filled with medieval medical tools and started feeling around the top of the marionette's head. "Remember how Madam M unlocked the box that held the Storm's secret letters? With a bobby pin!" She pulled one triumphantly from the marionette's hair. "We'll have to thank your sister later. I'll just take a quick look around—maybe there's something in there that will tell us where he went."

Don't leave me here, Chance thought frantically. But Penny couldn't hear him because she wasn't touching his strings. On purpose, maybe. He had the distinct feeling she was enjoying herself and didn't want to feel guilty about it.

No, he was just being paranoid again. Breaking into an office would be a lot harder holding a life-size marionette. She was being practical, that was all. Chance watched Penny kneel in front of the office door and begin jiggling the pin around in the lock. The resulting rattle sounded unusually loud in the silent museum.

It'll be fine, Chance reassured himself. *Even if she doesn't find anything now, we can just talk to Fortunato in the morning. Mom and Dad will be busy with the movers, and they won't—*

A shifting in the shadows halted Chance's thoughts.

The man with the sharp face stepped forward silently, any rustle or footstep lost to the sounds of Penny fiddling with the lock. The way he moved was slightly stilted, like his bones ached.

PENNY, LOOK OUT! Chance could scream in his head all he wanted, but she would never hear him.

Besides, it wasn't Penny whom the man was walking toward.

He leaned over until he was nose to nose with the marionette, and fear seized Chance in a way that would have rendered him paralyzed if he'd had the ability to move.

Up close, the man's face was even more striking. His eyes were a blue so light that when he tilted his head just so, they almost appeared white. The structure of his face was all sharp angles, the skin pulled tight over a skull with no curves. An ugly wart stood out on his otherwise smooth neck, like a gnarled knot on a tree. Gently he reached out a long, slender finger and touched the string at Chance's wrist.

Who are you? Chance thought as loudly and bravely as he could.

The man smiled.

I am your puppeteer.

Chance barely had time to register the fact that the man had spoken without opening his mouth, before he lifted the marionette and the spindle off the case and carried them over to the sealed-shut oak cabinet. When he touched the door, the wood shimmered and glowed as if lit up from within, and it opened.

It *opened*.

For a fraction of a second, Chance forgot his plight. Fortunato hadn't been lying—this cabinet really was *the* cabinet, the one that held the cabinetmaker's chambers! Chance stared eagerly, fully expecting to see a maze of cabinets spread out to infinity.

Yet inside was nothing but darkness.

The puppeteer stepped into the cabinet and turned around to face the museum. Chance caught a final glimpse of his own body—an eleven-year-old boy in his pajamas, loudly jiggling a bobby pin in a lock, oblivious to the horrors behind him.

As the puppeteer closed the cabinet door, Chance wondered if he would ever see himself again.

READY FOR AN ADVENTURE

"It's not working." Penny stood and studied the bobby pin, which was now crooked and useless. The Storm had never actually explained *how* Madam M used a pin to unlock the box. Apparently, shoving it into the lock and randomly wiggling it wasn't the way. "We need a new plan," Penny decided, turning around and walking back to the case. "I think . . ." She stopped and blinked.

The marionette and the spindle were gone.

Instinctively, Penny glanced up at her old spot on the shelf. It too was empty.

Chance was *gone.*

But that was impossible. Penny turned full circle, listening and looking. The museum was as still and silent as ever. Wait, there *was* a sound: a rhythmic *thump-thump, thump-thump, thump-thump.* . . .

Her heart. Well, Chance's heart. She could feel it pounding hard and loud in his chest. This, Penny knew, was a moment when a real person would experience fear and panic. And because she was in a real body, she was feeling the symptoms. A racing heartbeat, a sinking sensation in her stomach, cold sweat dampening her palms.

All these feelings made Penny want to run. And so she did.

She sprinted to the front of the museum, leaping over boxes and knocking over a stack of books. She burst through the door and stood panting on the sidewalk, looking up and down the street.

It was deserted.

Penny gritted her teeth. She was not a panicky, irrational boy. She was a marionette, capable of calm and rational thought.

If someone had taken Chance, that person had not left the museum. Yet.

Penny turned and walked back inside, pulling the door closed and locking it. Then she headed back to her shelf.

Penny had spent all the life she could remember staring at this area of the museum from her spot. She knew every inch of it. So a quick assessment of her surroundings was all she needed to see that the missing marionette was not the only thing out of place.

The door to the oak cabinet, which had always been sealed shut, was now open just a crack.

Penny marched up to it, yanked the door open, and stared inside.

It was empty.

Penny frowned, stepping inside and feeling around the dark corners just to be certain. But the cabinet contained nothing but a smell, one that vaguely reminded Penny of the buttery rolls Mrs. Bonvillain had served with dinner, but brighter and crisper. It was an odd smell for the interior of a cabinet, Penny thought. She started to climb out and slipped.

Grabbing the door, she looked down and saw a piece of paper she hadn't noticed in the darkness. She picked it up and turned it over.

★ ★ ★ Step right up! ★ ★ ★
DREAMLAND TRAVELING CARNIVAL

- ★ Rides for the Young, and the Young at Heart!
- ★ Delicious Foods Like You've Never Tasted!
- ★ Penny Arcade and Other Games of Skill and Chance!
- ★ Sideshow Performers and Vaudeville Acts!
- ★ Puppet Shows with Adventure and Danger!
- ★ And Much, Much More!
- ★ When: Every Day, June Through August
- ★ Where: City Park

Penny read every word of the flyer twice. She didn't need the Storm to tell her that this was a clue. In fact, it was such a perfect clue, it almost seemed too good to be true. As if it had been left on purpose.

She folded the flyer and stuffed it in her pajama pocket. So the thief had taken Chance to the carnival through this cabinet. It made perfect sense—after all, hadn't Fortunato always said the cabinetmaker's creations possessed magical properties? Just to be sure, Penny investigated the rest of the museum, checking behind every shelf and inside every trunk. Then she went back up the stairs to the second floor and knocked on the door to Fortunato's apartment for several minutes. She considered picking the lock, but this door had a double bolt. At last, defeated, Penny trudged up to the Bonvillains' apartment. She crawled into Chance's bed and gazed at the ceiling.

The guilt she'd felt earlier that day, when she'd experienced the joy of mopping while Chance was trapped and helpless, was nothing compared with this. This guilt washed over her in gradually increasing waves until she was drowning in it, and she opened her mouth to breathe in and out. She needed to focus.

The man with the sharp face—for it had to have been him—had stolen the marionette. A kidnapping, Penny realized, like the episode where one of Madam M's henchmen had taken the mayor's child for ransom. Penny remembered how terrified the young actress voicing the part of the child had sounded. She wondered if Chance felt that terrified now.

But she knew where to find him. The carnival. The man with the sharp face had wanted Penny to find that flyer; she was sure of it. Just like he'd wanted Chance to use that spindle, knowing it would cause them to swap.

If this were *Storm at Dawn,* an exciting quest would ensue, in which Penny would set off on her own to the carnival and engage in an exhilarating fight scene with the villain before rescuing Chance.

However, this was not a radio show. And Penny was far too logical to walk right into a villain's trap alone.

The smart, though less glamorous, thing to do would be to tell the Bonvillains the truth. Then they could go to the carnival together, perhaps with police accompanying them, and demand that the man return Chance. Afterward, they would find Fortunato, who would swap Penny and Chance back to their rightful bodies.

This was Penny's plan. It was not the most romantic of plans, but it was a smart one, and she drifted off to sleep feeling fairly confident.

The next morning, though, things did not go according to plan.

For starters, Mrs. Bonvillain woke her far earlier than Penny wanted to be woken. She had never slept before, and had dreamed of spinning and laughing on a dance floor while the band onstage played faster and faster. Her skirt had twirled and her shoes had tap-tap-tapped on the hard-wood and her hair had been loose, black curls flying out as she spun. A melody had wrapped around her like silk: a woman's voice, husky with laughter.

In her dream, she had been back in her marionette body. But there had been no hands holding her strings.

Now Penny sat up in bed and examined Chance's arms, then wiggled Chance's legs. This was a perfectly nice body too, but it wasn't hers. It wasn't uncomfortable, but it didn't quite fit right. Maybe that would make it easier to swap back when the time came.

That was what she told herself as she dressed in Chance's clothes. But deep down, the truth was that living inside this body was still infinitely better than a puppet shell.

When Penny joined the rest of the family in the kitchen, she intended to launch right into the matter at hand. No sense wasting time. But Mr. Bonvillain was on the phone, and Mrs. Bonvillain kept darting in and out of the kitchen to check on the movers as they carried the furniture and boxes down to their truck. Penny sat across from Constance and ate cereal for the first time (crunchy at first, then mushy, and far too sweet). When a loud thud and muffled curse came from the stairwell, Mr. and Mrs. Bonvillain both swiveled around and stared at the door. Then they hurried out of the kitchen, muttering things about "better not be my fine china" and "not worth what they're charging."

Constance drained her glass of milk and wiped her mouth primly on a napkin. Then she smiled at Penny.

"So," she said. "Who are you?"

Penny swallowed another mouthful of sugary mush too soon and coughed. "Huh?"

"Who are you?" Constance repeated. "I know my own brother when I see him." She leaned across the table, her eyes bright with curiosity. "Or is it that your soul is missing? Like in *The Cabinetmaker's Apprentice*? Did Penny take your soul, Chance?"

"I most certainly did not," Penny said indignantly. "We swapped. And it's his fault, if you want to know the truth."

Constance tilted her head. "Swapped?"

"Yes. I'm Penny. Chance's soul is in the marionette."

"Ah." Constance nodded. "Okay, I understand. Sorry about that. I didn't realize marionettes had souls."

"I didn't say I have a soul."

"Well, you must," Constance said matter-of-factly. "Some part of you is in my brother's body."

Penny had not even considered this, and she mulled it over for several seconds. She had to admit, it was a logical conclusion. "Well," she said at last. "If marionettes do have souls, then that dumb old story makes even less sense. Because the whole point was that marionettes needed souls in order to come to life."

"That's true," Constance agreed. "And Chance's soul didn't bring your marionette body to life, did it?"

"No."

"Interesting."

Penny stared at the girl. Her face was so earnest and open. "Aren't you upset? Your brother is trapped inside a puppet."

"I was upset yesterday," Constance admitted. "I knew something was wrong."

"You didn't seem upset."

Chance's sister smiled. "Yes. I'm good at hiding it. I'm very upset right now, in fact. But now that I know what happened, I can work on fixing it."

Penny returned the smile. She was struck by the sudden need to win this girl's approval.

"I will tell your parents about this," Penny said magnanimously. "I tried already, but they're very busy."

Constance laughed. "Now, why would you do a thing like that? They'll never believe you."

"Why not?" Penny asked. "You knew as soon as you looked at me that I wasn't Chance."

For the first time, a shadow passed over Constance's cheery face. "Yes, well. I don't think my parents would see the difference. They don't look at us that closely."

"Oh," said Penny. "I hope we can convince them. We'll need their help to get Chance back."

At this, Constance sat up straight. "Get him back? Where is he?"

And so Penny told Constance the whole story. She half

expected the girl to fall to pieces when she learned her brother's soul had been stolen by the villainous man with the sharp face. Constance was very nice, but her sweet voice and girlish looks reminded Penny strongly of the simpering female characters on *Storm at Dawn,* the pretty ones who broke down and cried when the slightest bit of danger presented itself. But Constance just listened intently. And when Penny showed her the flyer, Constance's face lit up.

"So the man with the sharp face took him to the carnival!" Constance exclaimed. "It says right here—puppet shows. All we have to do now is rescue him."

"Exactly," Penny said. "Do you think you can get your parents to believe us?"

Constance waved dismissively. "Oh, we aren't telling them. They can't know anything about this."

"But—"

"Penny," Constance interrupted, her tone gentle but firm. "You don't know my parents. They were very upset that my brother wanted to keep you in the first place. If they hear him talk about swapping souls with a doll by using some piece of a magical spinning wheel, they'll think you're loony. No, really, they would take you to a head doctor. Trust me. They'll never help us with this. We have to do it alone."

"Okay." Penny clasped her hands on the table. "I think the man with the sharp face left that flyer for me to find.

See? He included my name, and Chance's, to make sure I knew it was deliberate."

"'Penny Arcade and Other Games of Skill and Chance,'" Constance read from the flyer. "Clever! Good catch."

"Thank you," Penny said, pleased. "But this means the man will be expecting a rescue. He'll be waiting for us. This is going to be dangerous. Are you sure you want to come?"

Giggling, Constance began clearing away the dishes.

Penny stared at her. "Well?"

Constance blinked. "Oh, you weren't joking?" Penny shook her head. Constance tossed their paper bowls and plastic spoons into the trash, then came around the table.

"The man with the sharp face might be expecting you, but he's not expecting me. And there is no villain in the world scary enough to stop me from getting my little brother back."

She said this with an easy smile, as if declaring her intent to pour another bowl of cereal rather than embark on a dangerous mission. And at the words *little brother,* Penny experienced another new emotion. A pulling in her chest, like a hand gently tugging at her heart, trying to get her attention.

"So," Constance continued, lowering her voice, "should we sneak out now, while my parents are distracted?"

"Yes," Penny agreed, and she followed Constance into the living room.

They were immediately confronted by a harried-looking Mrs. Bonvillain. She took each child by the arm and led them back to their bedrooms, her words spilling out so fast they left no room for protest.

"The movers have emptied your rooms. Please do one last check for anything left behind, and be sure to look in the closets. Don't forget to use the bathroom before we go— your father would prefer not to stop on the way to Daystar Meadows, and there might be traffic. Be in the foyer in five minutes."

"Okay! Would you mind if Chance and I got a bottle of soda for the car ride first?" Constance asked politely. "We can just run across the street; we'll be right back."

"Your father's already taken care of snacks!" Mrs. Bonvillain gently pushed each of them into their separate rooms. "Hurry, now!"

Sighing, Penny checked Chance's closet, then took a quick glance around his room, which was barren. She was about to head over to Constance's room when her gaze drifted to the window. More specifically, to the alley across the street, where the silhouette of a man was visible. When Penny moved forward, the man stepped back into the shadows. But not before Penny recognized him.

"Constance, hurry!" she called, running out of the room and down the hall without waiting to see if Constance was following. Penny thundered down the stairs, burst through the door, and plowed right into Mr. Bonvillain. A second later, someone slammed into her from behind.

"Whoa there!" Mr. Bonvillain laughed, stepping back. "Glad to see you two are so ready to go." Penny glanced at Constance, who was breathing heavily but still smiling at her father as if nothing were wrong. He handed each of them a bottle of soda—root beer for Penny, cherry cola for Constance—then gestured to the blue sedan pulled up along the curb in front of the moving truck. "Our chariot awaits!"

"But . . . we . . ." Penny cast a desperate glance at the now-empty alley, then at Constance. "Can I just, um . . ."

Mrs. Bonvillain spoke up from behind her, her voice bright in a forced way. "Are we all ready?"

"All ready!" her husband replied, his tone matching hers. He marched over to the sedan and pulled the back door open, gesturing grandly. "After you, my dear," he said to Constance, who let out a tinkling little laugh. Penny shot her a look, hoping her expression conveyed the urgency she was feeling. But Constance just slid into the backseat, looking as though she didn't have a care in the world.

"Come on, Chance!" she called.

Gritting her teeth, Penny forced herself to get into the car. As soon as Mr. Bonvillain closed the door, she rounded on Constance. "I saw Fortunato," she hissed. "He's here! He's right over there, and he *saw* me. We can't just leave! He can—"

"We have to." Constance leaned forward, watching as the Bonvillains spoke to the movers. "It's too late. But don't worry, Penny. I have an idea."

Before Penny could respond, Mr. and Mrs. Bonvillain slid into the front seats and slammed their doors in unison. They both turned, beaming at their children.

"Ready for an adventure?" Mrs. Bonvillain asked.

"Yes!" Constance cried, clapping her hands.

"I guess," Penny mumbled.

The engine roared to life, Mr. Bonvillain pulled the car away from the curb, and they were off.

Penny watched out the back window as the Museum of the Peculiar Arts disappeared. This should have been exciting. She was in a car. After spending her whole life never leaving the museum, she was about to leave the *city*. But Penny was too upset to feel any other emotion. When she faced the front again, Mrs. Bonvillain was fiddling with the radio knobs.

"How about a little music?"

A few seconds later, the reedy, familiar sound of a saxophone filled the car. Penny's eyes widened, and she squeezed her hands in her lap. She recognized this song. She heard it often on *Live from Club Heavenly Blues,* and it was her favorite. When the singer joined in, Penny's breath caught in her throat.

"Every time it rains, it rains pennies from heaven.
Don't you know each cloud contains pennies from heaven?"

The woman's voice was husky yet sweet, the same voice Penny heard every night on the radio. The same voice from her dream.

A hand on her arm made her jump. Penny stared at Constance, who was watching her with obvious concern.

"Are you okay?" Constance whispered, softly enough that her parents couldn't hear.

"Yes." Penny was surprised at how Chance's voice came out, all cracked and hoarse. In fact, his throat was very tight. And his eyes felt as though they were on fire. She wondered briefly if she had broken Chance's body somehow.

Blinking rapidly, Penny turned to watch the city pass by through the window. As the song ended, a tear, her first real tear, slipped down her cheek.

ENDLESS PATIENCE

Dreamland Traveling Carnival had a way of feeling permanent despite its name. Perhaps it was the speed with which it was set up and torn down. It would arrive the first Saturday morning of June, rides and vendors speckled throughout the park as if they had always been there. Then the last Sunday morning of August, the sun would rise over a quiet, empty park, the heady smells of hot oil and sugar and popcorn still lingering in the air.

The puppeteer's trailer did not appear until the second week of August, and it caused a fresh wave of excitement. It had no windows, but an impressive stage jutted out in front, its shiny dark red curtain, which fluttered in the breeze, ready to rise at any moment. The walls were covered in doors of all shapes and sizes: round, oval, square, rectangular, even a hexagonal one so small a cat would have a hard time squeezing through. The trailer was made of all sorts of wood: spalted maple and mesquite, sycamore and holly, Russian olive and Brazilian cherry. It was a random patchwork of beiges and reds and browns, and no matter how long you stared at it, the pattern never quite settled, a subtle kaleidoscope that shifted when you blinked. Children stopped and gaped as if under some spell. Adults made jokes about its odd appearance to cover the fact that it made them feel vaguely uncomfortable, like a house made of candy with the silhouette of a witch lurking on the other side of the spun-sugar window.

Some remembered the puppeteer from their youth, although no one had laid eyes on him in ages. Many of them, young and old, had heard the rumors. Children peered around their parents' legs to gaze longingly at the stage, and the older ones dared each other to run up and peek behind the curtain. When the puppeteer emerged from around the back of the trailer, carrying a sign, a hush fell momentarily. Then the whispers began.

"He looks so young! Doesn't he?"

"Exactly how my grandpa described him!"

"That's not *him,* though. It can't be the same one—he'd be ancient."

"Do you think they're related?"

The puppeteer's lips curved upward as he walked to the stage. His bones and joints were stiffer than ever, but he ignored the discomfort and moved as elegantly as he could. The pain would be over soon enough. He hung the sign below the stage, then stepped out of the way to let the crowd read it.

———— THE AMAZING ————
PRINCESS PENNY PUPPET SHOW
★ ★ ★ ★ ★ ★ ★ ★ ★ ★ ★ ★ ★
Shows every hour, on the hour!
Starting tomorrow at 10:00 a.m.!

The children's eyes lit up, and the excited chatter began. Satisfied, the puppeteer walked around to the back of the trailer. Once away from prying eyes, he grimaced and stretched his aching arms. Then he pushed a small patch of ash wood, and a door concealed by the mishmash pattern opened.

The puppeteer stepped inside and closed the door quietly. The real Penny, he knew, would soon be on her way to rescue the damsel in distress. It would take some time for her to arrive, but the puppeteer had endless patience. And besides, time was necessary for Penny to come to terms with what she needed to do, and for Chance to accept his fate.

For now, the puppeteer had a show to prepare.

A WONDERFUL BIG SISTER

Daystar Meadows was more terrible than Penny could ever have imagined.

She could see it sprawled below them as the sedan reached the peak of the bridge that crossed the river. Rows upon rows of identical houses, all curved upward like bland smiles. When she turned back to look at the hazy skyline across the water, she thought the city might as well have been across the ocean.

After exiting the bridge, the Bonvillains drove down Main Street. The buildings were fairly uniform; even their signs were in the same curly typeface: POST OFFICE. GROCERY. SEAFOOD RESTAURANT.

It became even more abhorrent when they entered the sea of houses. Penny stared through the window, aghast at the sameness of it all. It was as if a magician had conjured one picture-perfect house, complete with too-green lawn and too-white fence, and then replicated it over and over again. Even the sunshine seemed fake.

She completely understood why Chance had chosen the carnival over this.

"Here we are!" Mr. Bonvillain said triumphantly, swinging the sedan into a driveway. "What do you think?" Everyone climbed out of the car and gathered together on the bright green grass. The house was painted yellow with white trim. There were empty flower boxes under the windows, and a straw welcome mat on the front stoop. The only thing differentiating it from the houses to the right and left was the silver-plated numbers 2323 next to the front door instead of 2321 and 2325.

"It's the prettiest house on the block!" exclaimed Mrs. Bonvillain.

Penny frowned. "What do you mean? It looks just like all the other houses."

At that, Mr. and Mrs. Bonvillain shared an exasperated look. Then the moving truck pulled up, and they hurried over to greet the movers. Constance nudged Penny with her elbow.

"You do a really great Chance impression! That's exactly what he would have said."

"Oh. Good." In all honesty, Penny had not thought much about whether or not she sounded like Chance. His parents had not given any indication that they suspected anything was different about their son. Perhaps Constance had been right. The Bonvillains did not look at their children beyond the surface.

The next several hours were dedicated to unpacking. While the movers did all the heavy lifting, Penny and Constance were kept busy unloading boxes of dishes and books and knickknacks. After that, Mrs. Bonvillain ordered them to their rooms, where they were to, as she put it, "set things up and make it feel like home." Penny folded Chance's clothes and put them in his dresser, made his bed with his blue plaid sheets and blanket, and shelved his books. Her delight upon finding a box labeled STORM AT DAWN quickly turned to disappointment when it contained only cheap plastic toys. Still, she placed each on Chance's bookshelf with as much care as Fortunato gave to his oddities.

Fortunato. Penny's brow furrowed as she recalled seeing the museum owner in the alley. He'd been so close, and she had failed to reach him.

She wondered why he hadn't answered his door last night. If he had, Chance would not have been taken, and they might have been swapped back by now.

Penny felt a surge of energy, most likely brought on by

guilt. She hurried down the hall to Constance's room, taking care to be quiet lest Mrs. Bonvillain find her and set her with yet another chore.

"Constance . . ." Penny stopped in the doorway, blinking.

The canopy bed in the corner featured a fluffy pink comforter, much of which was covered in various stuffed animals. The dresser was painted white and included a vanity mirror and a dainty stool, while paintings of flowers and horses adorned the walls. It seemed as though everything, from the lampshades to the little pillows on her bed, was covered in frills. The effect was overwhelming.

Constance looked up from a box of books. "Are you finished unpacking?" she asked, and then, without waiting for a response, waved a book at her. "Look what I found!" Penny crossed the room and took the book. It was fairly thin and bore the title *The Cabinetmaker's Apprentice*. Constance laughed at the exasperated look Penny gave her. "It's still a good story, even if it's not true. It's always been my favorite book, actually."

"Oh." Penny handed it back, mildly surprised. She would have expected Constance's favorite book to involve fairies or princesses or some such, not evil puppets. She watched as Constance tucked the book inside a small knapsack, which also contained a change of clothes and a coin purse. Constance zipped up the knapsack and got to her feet.

"Did you pack a bag?"

Penny blinked. "No. I unpacked, like your mother said to."

"Yes, but I mean for our trip back into the city." When Penny just blinked again, Constance crossed the room and closed her door. "We *are* going back to rescue Chance, aren't we?"

"Of course! That's why I came in here, to come up with a plan."

"There's a train that runs from Daystar Meadows into the financial district," Constance replied promptly. "That's how my father is going to get to and from work every day." She pointed to a small brochure on her dresser. "His train schedule. I saw it in the car and took it when no one was looking. The last train for the city departs at quarter to midnight." Penny opened her mouth, but Constance plowed ahead. "I know, I know, that means we'll be wandering around the city in the middle of the night, and it would be safer to wait for the morning train. But if we leave as soon as my parents are asleep, that gives us a huge head start."

"I wasn't going to argue," Penny said when the girl finally paused for breath. "Leaving tonight is a great plan. Where's the train station?"

"There's a map in that brochure," Constance explained. "It's two blocks north of Main Street, which isn't even a mile from here. I have enough money for our tickets, plus some extra for food. You should pack a change of clothes, and we'll take some fruit and crackers, too."

Penny nodded, studying the girl's face. Her eyes were bright with excitement, but not in the way they were around her parents. It was a very subtle difference, but Penny could see it now. Constance's enthusiasm for Daystar Meadows had been forced. This was genuine.

"You're looking forward to this," Penny blurted out as realization dawned. "Even though it's dangerous."

Constance's smile turned slightly shifty. "Well, maybe a little," she admitted. "It's going to be a real adventure, isn't it? I've never had one before."

"I suppose so," Penny said. She felt a little spark in her chest at the thought.

Because unpacking left little time for cooking, dinner was sandwiches. Penny was pleased about this and slathered heaps of peanut butter on her bread. When Chance's parents left the kitchen, she and Constance made two extra sandwiches to take with them that night. Afterward Penny took a bath, put on a pair of pajamas, and said good night to Mr. and Mrs. Bonvillain. Then she changed back into regular clothes and sat on Chance's bed.

Now it was simply a matter of waiting, something marionettes were very good at. Penny gazed at the wall. Soon this would be her life again. Sitting and staring. Although she was sure Chance would move her around frequently.

Still, nothing compared with being able to move on one's own.

At eleven o'clock on the nose, the door to Chance's room opened quietly, and Constance slipped inside. Penny stood, picking up the backpack filled with sandwiches and a change of clothes and comic books. "Why are you dressed like that?" she whispered.

Constance looked down at herself. She wore a bright green dress with white polka dots, a rounded collar, and a pleated skirt. Her light brown hair was curled and pulled back with shiny barrettes.

"This is my traveling outfit," she replied. "My mother bought it for me when we took the train upstate in the spring."

"It's not very practical for sneaking out." Penny gestured at her own outfit: jeans, a gray T-shirt, and sneakers. "The Storm recommends dark colors and comfortable shoes. And a mask, depending on the situation. I don't think we need masks, though."

Constance beamed. "Oh, I didn't know you listened to *Storm at Dawn*! Well, you can dress like him if you want. I'm going to dress like me. Besides, my mother would kill me if I went out wearing that."

Penny thought that was a strange thing to be concerned about, considering Mrs. Bonvillain would surely be more upset over the fact that her daughter had run away than over her choice of runaway attire. But Penny just shrugged and followed Constance out of the room.

They tiptoed down the carpeted hall, through the living room, and to the front door. When Penny reached for Chance's blue key ring hanging next to the other sets, Constance placed a hand on her arm and shook her head. Once they were outside and the door was closed, Constance pulled back the welcome mat to reveal a spare key.

"I saw Dad put this here right before dinner," she told Penny as she locked the door, then returned the key. "If he notices our keys are missing when he leaves for work at six-thirty, they'll figure out we're gone. This buys us a few more hours."

Penny was impressed.

After consulting the map in the train brochure, they set off down the quiet residential street. As they walked, Constance kept up a stream of whispered conversation, most of which was about how Daystar Meadows differed from the city. After nearly ten minutes of this, Penny asked, "Do you like it better here?"

Constance hesitated. "I like both."

"That's not what I asked," Penny said. "If you could choose to live here or in the city, which would you pick?"

"Well . . ." Constance looked around the deserted street nervously. "Honestly? The city," she admitted. "But don't tell my parents that!"

"Chance did," Penny said. "He told them he didn't want to move."

"I know, and it upset them," Constance said. "Plus, it's different with Chance. He's always been that way."

"What way?"

"Kind of negative, I guess. I don't mean that in a bad way," Constance added quickly. "Really, he's a lot more honest than I am. I'd rather keep my parents happy, so I don't complain."

"You lie to them?"

Constance's eyes widened. "No!"

"But you just said—"

"There's the station!" Constance said, quickening her pace. While she didn't seem at all upset, Penny had the distinct impression she wanted to end the conversation.

The Daystar Meadows train station was small but unsurprisingly spotless. While it was by no means crowded, a few dozen people were milling up and down the platform. On a nearby bench, an older couple sat looking through brochures, and a young woman stood not far away, bent over a stroller and making cooing noises.

A security guard eyed Penny and Constance as they approached the ticket booth. Constance glanced at him before turning to the woman behind the glass and pulling out her coin purse.

"Hi!" she said in her perkiest voice. "Two tickets for the next train, please." She slid the money under the glass, and

the woman pushed two tickets forward without responding. "Thank you!" Constance took Penny by the arm and
whispered: "Follow my lead."

Penny allowed herself to be pulled over to the bench,
where Constance promptly sat next to the older couple and
motioned for Penny to sit as well. The woman, who had a
kind face and perfectly coiffed gray hair, glanced up.

"Hello!" Constance said. "Are you moving to Daystar
Meadows?" She gestured to the brochures, which Penny
realized were for houses just like the Bonvillains'.

"We're considering it," the woman said. Her smile was
kind but her eyes were sad.

"So quiet out here," the man added, stifling a yawn.
"Very peaceful."

Very boring, Penny wanted to say, but she didn't. Instead,
she nudged Constance and gave her a questioning look. But
Constance ignored her.

"We just moved out here," she said. "It's wonderful!
You'll love it."

A bell began to chime, and there was a hissing sound
as the train doors opened. The couple got to their feet, and
Constance followed suit, grabbing Penny's hand tightly.
Penny saw her glance once or twice more at the security
guard while maintaining a constant stream of chatter.

"Don't you just love riding the train? Our parents took
us upstate a few months ago, and the views were beautiful
once we got out of the city. We stayed in this adorable little

town in the middle of nowhere, and there was a lake, and we went hiking and . . ."

She continued this way as they boarded the train. Penny couldn't help noticing that the man's smile had become rather fixed, while the woman appeared to be enjoying Constance's cheery jabbering. In fact, she invited them to sit in the seats across from her and her husband, at which point Penny distinctly saw him roll his eyes.

"I think you're bothering that man," Penny whispered to Constance as they stuffed their bags into the overhead apartment.

"Oh, I know," Constance whispered back. "But that security guard was watching us, and I wanted him to think we were with our grandparents. Otherwise he might report two kids taking the train into the city in the middle of the night, you know?"

"Ah."

Penny sat back in her seat. It occurred to her that her rescue mission would have been over before it had begun if it weren't for Constance. It was Constance who had known what would happen if Penny told the Bonvillains the truth. It was Constance who had found the train schedule and formed a plan to sneak out successfully. It was Constance who had stopped them from getting caught by a security guard at the station.

Penny had thought of Constance as the typical early victim in an episode of *Storm at Dawn*: pretty, sweet, and thoroughly unprepared. But Constance was obviously quite capable. And there was something else, too. Something in the way Constance had taken Penny's hand and squeezed it protectively as they walked past the security guard. That familiar feeling Penny couldn't name but was starting to like very much.

Safety. That wasn't the whole feeling, but it was part of it. Her eyelids drooped, and she rested her head on Constance's shoulder.

"You're obviously a wonderful big sister," she heard the woman tell Constance. The last thing Penny felt before she drifted asleep was a light *thump-thump* in her chest.

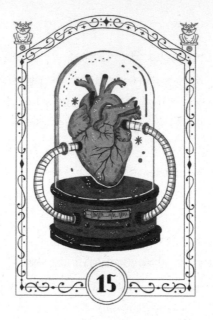

A MUCH BETTER MATCH

The inside of the puppeteer's trailer was covered in doors.

Not just on the walls, but on the floor and ceiling, too. All different types of wood, all polished to a gleam. It should have been pretty, but all Chance could think was that the trailer was made of puppet skin.

He did not remember anything between the puppeteer hiding in Fortunato's cabinet back at the museum and arriving here. The cabinet door had closed, all had gone black, and then a different door had opened and Chance had found himself sitting in a cupboard overlooking the trailer's interior. He hadn't even known it was a trailer at first, and he'd wondered if he was looking at a small part of the cabinetmaker's legendary chambers after all.

It wasn't until the puppeteer had opened the door to outside and Chance had caught an achingly familiar glimpse of a Ferris wheel over the trees in the distance, accompanied by the sounds of shrieking laughter, that Chance realized where he was. He could not smell, because he was a marionette, but he knew the air must be thick with the scent of popcorn and cotton candy. The Bonvillains lived—*had* lived—only a few blocks from this park. Chance and Constance had spent nearly every day at the carnival last summer, and every other summer Chance could remember.

The fact that he knew exactly where he was yet could do nothing to escape made every passing second torturous. It was easier to forget.

And that was exactly what Chance's mind began to do. Slowly, so slowly he didn't notice it at first, the fog crept into his mind and began swallowing his earliest memories—the ones that were already a bit hazy. He allowed it to happen. Forgetting made the pain of loss easier to bear.

He spent most of his time pondering the cabinets and their contents. One in particular. While most of the other cabinets simply stored the puppeteer's tools, this one contained a spinning wheel, sitting in the dark.

Even motionless, it fascinated Chance: the shiny spokes of the wooden wheel, the metallic pedals, the polished spindle—the very same spindle the puppeteer had slipped into Chance's mail, now reattached. It dawned on Chance again how strange it was that Penny would even recognize a spindle. After all, there were no spinning wheels in the museum.

When the cabinet door was open, Chance would stare at the wheel for hours, his mind filled with fairy tales about greedy men spinning straw into gold, or princesses pricking their fingers and falling into a forever sleep.

He wondered what wickedness the puppeteer used his spinning wheel to perform. Because while the rest of his tools—knives and nails and screwdrivers of all sorts—had a clear purpose, Chance could not imagine what good a spinning wheel would be in the business of building marionettes.

Not that Chance had actually witnessed any marionette-building. He was grateful for that. He did not like imagining their parts strewn about, legs and arms and hollow heads.

The first time someone knocked on the trailer door, the puppeteer closed Chance's cabinet before answering. A moment later Chance heard the muffled sound of a new voice. Another person was in the trailer.

Chance thought he had experienced the height of frustration when the puppeteer first kidnapped him. But now it increased tenfold. Worse was knowing that even if the visitor did happen upon Chance, all he would see was a pretty marionette, not a boy desperately in need of help.

He could hear them clearly. The newcomer's voice could not have contrasted more with the puppeteer's. It was warm and low and gravelly and made Chance feel safe. Or at least it made him remember what safety felt like.

The puppeteer's voice was empty. Chance could think of no other word. It wasn't particularly high or low, nor was it more smooth than scratchy. It was just vocal cords vibrating, teeth and lips coming together and breaking apart, a tongue moving between them. No anger, no fear, no emotion whatsoever. Fortunately, the puppeteer did not speak out loud very often.

"Ah, yes, I remember these tools," the new voice said. Chance could hear doors and drawers opening and closing, the rattle of carving knives and the skittering of nails and screws.

"They're quite powerful," the puppeteer replied, and if wood could break out in goose bumps, Chance's marionette arms and legs would have been covered in them. "But then, you already knew that."

There was a pause, the heavy kind during which words are being carefully weighed before spoken.

"They are indeed good tools," the new voice replied at last. "But the real magic comes from the hands that wield them. That's what Papa always said."

Chance tried to imagine what this person looked like based on his voice. *His* because he sounded like a man, and a somewhat older one at that. He would have kind eyes and more than a few wrinkles, and though he would be smiling, it would be a smile born of nerves, not happiness. Chance's imagination began to sketch in the details. Silver hair and a salt-and-pepper beard, eyes like coal beneath bushy gray brows, and . . . wait. Had he said *Papa*?

In his mind, Chance frowned. He was not painting a new picture. He was digging up an old photograph. An image of someone he once knew very well.

When his cabinet door opened, Chance found himself gazing into familiar charcoal eyes. The name drifted up in his mind as if from the bottom of a deep well.

Fortunato!

The former museum owner sighed and tilted his head, caterpillar brows furrowed. More memories rushed to the surface now, so clear that Chance was seized with alarm that the fog had obscured them so quickly. *Help me!* he cried, willing his friend to hear his thoughts. *I'm not Penny, we swapped bodies, you have to take me with you, please—*

"The real magic," the puppeteer said, and now his tone was mocking. Fortunato did not turn to look at him, but his eyes flashed with an emotion Chance couldn't place. Fear? Anger? It could have been either, or both. "Your precious papa did love to say that, didn't he? He couldn't stand the thought of people finding out that anyone could work his magic with wood. That it wasn't his skills but his tools."

A muscle twitched in Fortunato's cheek, but still he did

112

not turn away from Chance. "I suspect this is a topic on which we will never agree."

"Indeed." The puppeteer smiled coldly. "As we learned from my many fruitless visits to your little museum. Well," he added thoughtfully, his gaze lingering on Chance, "not entirely fruitless, as it turned out."

Fortunato faced the puppeteer. "I've changed my mind," he said abruptly. "I never should have agreed to this. Even if you do have Nicolette, even if you're telling the truth about the chambers, I can't . . ."

He trailed off when the puppeteer withdrew something from the deep pocket of his cloak. A ribbon, pale pink and faded with age. The sight of it caused the blood to drain from Fortunato's face. His lips trembled when he spoke.

"Is that . . . is it . . ."

"Nicolette's, of course," the puppeteer murmured. "I have not lied to you. The chambers were not destroyed in the great fire, nor was she."

Fortunato squeezed his eyes closed, tears streaming down his wrinkled cheeks.

"She will be yours, as will the chambers," the puppeteer continued. "Once you have helped me see this through. The plan is already in motion, Fortunato. It's too late to back out now."

"I'll make the sacrifice instead," Fortunato choked out. "Please, let me. You can't ask the boy to . . ."

He stopped because the puppeteer was laughing again.

"How very noble. Sadly, I am not interested in what you have to give, Fortunato." He slipped the ribbon back into his pocket and strode over to the cabinet that held the spinning wheel. He pulled open the door, then stepped inside and lifted something off the floor. The cabinet was dark, the outline of the spinning wheel barely visible, but Chance was hit with the sudden impression that the lack of light concealed the true size of the interior.

The puppeteer emerged with another marionette in his arms, and all thoughts of the cabinet's size flew from Chance's mind. This marionette was dressed as a knight, complete with silver helmet and sword.

"Nearly finished," the puppeteer said. "It takes time for the wood to settle." His lips curled as if he had told a joke. Fortunato did not laugh. In fact, he recoiled at the sight of the puppet.

The puppeteer chuckled. "Oh, come now. You're a grown man, are you not?"

Without waiting for a response, the puppeteer flipped up the silver visor to reveal the top half of the marionette's face, and Chance stared in awe. This was how he'd felt the first time he saw Penny. A pair of brown eyes gazed back at him, obviously glass, yet so real that Chance could swear the puppet was just as curious about him as he was about it. The knight had been made from a darker type of wood than Penny, and the eyelashes were a bit thicker.

Turning, the puppeteer held the knight up next to

Chance. His gaze moved to the shelf below them, then back again. "Marvelous," he whispered. "All of them."

All of them.

This took a moment to sink in. There were more marionettes below Chance, as well as the knight now at his side. His mind whirled. If Penny could think and talk, maybe these puppets could too.

Suddenly, Chance felt a little less lonely.

"I'll admit, after so many failed attempts, I was beginning to lose hope," the puppeteer told Fortunato softly. "But your apprentice is a much better match than any of these would have been. His coloring, in particular."

Chance puzzled over this. Fortunato's apprentice . . . was the puppeteer talking about *him*? What was he a match for?

"Nicolette," Fortunato replied, his voice breaking slightly. He kept his gaze averted from the marionettes, as if the sight of them pained or frightened him. "Where is Nicolette?"

The puppeteer's thin brow quirked up. "I'll return her when your apprentice"—here his eyes flickered over to Chance—"does as you promised he would."

Fortunato swallowed. Nodded.

"He will."

"He must," the puppeteer whispered.

Chance stared hard at Fortunato, as if he could find the meaning of this bizarre conversation written in his wrinkles. He remembered the hesitant look on the old man's face when he'd offered Penny to Chance, as if he'd wanted

Chance to say no. As if he'd known what the puppeteer was planning. As if he were a villain's accomplice.

But that was impossible. Fortunato would never put Chance in such danger.

The puppeteer took the knight marionette and carried it back into the spinning-wheel cabinet. Fortunato hesitated, eyeing the door. Then he hurried over to Chance's cupboard and leaned close, so close that their noses nearly touched. And he whispered:

"I'm so sorry. I swear, I will fix this, Chance."

He closed the cupboard door, and Chance was swallowed in darkness once more.

A LITTLE RISK

The train whistle screamed, jerking Penny from her sleep. She blinked, momentarily disoriented, and saw through the window that they were pulling into another stop. In the seat next to her, Constance smiled and held a finger to her lips.

"Don't wake the Goldsteins," she whispered, pointing. Mrs. Goldstein's head leaned against the window, her eyes closed. Next to her, Mr. Goldstein was snoring lightly, his mouth open wide enough that Penny could see his tonsils. She rubbed her eyes.

"Are we close?"

"Less than fifteen minutes, according to the schedule," Constance replied after glancing at her watch. Her cheeks flushed a bit when she noticed Penny staring at the book open in her lap: *The Cabinetmaker's Apprentice.*

"Is that really your favorite book?" Penny asked.

"Yes. Why?"

"It's just . . ." Penny shrugged. "I would've thought you'd like fairy tales more. Fortunato has a massive book filled with them. Stories about princesses and knights, witches and wizards, that sort of thing."

Constance wrinkled her nose. "Princesses and knights are fine, but they're a bit predictable, aren't they? All that swooning and unnecessary bravado."

"I suppose," Penny agreed.

"And witches and wizards are even worse," Constance went on. "The witches are always up to evil doings, and the wizards are always wise and benevolent. I've never liked those stories."

"Why not?"

"I just don't think it's fair," Constance said, "that boys with magic are written as exceptionally smart, but girls with magic are written as exceptionally mean." She patted the book in her lap. "Demon puppets, though, now that's an exciting story."

"I'm not a demon, you know," Penny told her. Her stomach felt twisted and tight.

Constance's response was a bit too quick. "Of course you're not. It's just . . ."

"What?"

Brows knit, Constance closed her book. "I know what you *aren't*," she whispered. "I want to know what you *are*."

"I'm a marionette." Penny had thought this much was clear. But Constance shook her head.

"You are, yes. But there are lots of marionettes in the world," Constance said gently. "And lots of people who pick them up and touch their strings, just like Chance did with you. If all those marionettes talked to all those people, everyone in the whole world would know about them."

Penny had to admit she had a point. "Well," she thought out loud, "maybe there are lots of marionettes in the world, but not all of them are lifelike."

Constance laughed. "Lifelike? You're more than that. You don't just *look* alive. You *are* alive."

The whistle screamed again. Mrs. Goldstein's eyelashes fluttered, and she yawned hugely. Her gaze moved from the darkness outside the window to Constance and Penny, and she smiled.

"Is someone picking you two up at the station?" she asked. "It's awfully late for anyone your age to be wandering around the city."

"Oh, yes," Constance said immediately. "Our parents will be there. Don't worry about us."

Penny noticed Mrs. Goldstein's brow arch skeptically, as if she found Constance's response less than reassuring. Constance must have seen it too, because her voice got slightly higher and her words tumbled out faster.

"Besides, we're used to this. We grew up in the city, you know. I took the train by myself for the first time when I was eight! It was only four stops, but still. And my brother knows the tracks inside and out—he's got maps of the whole city in his brain, honestly. I remember one time we were on a train heading downtown, but the conductor switched routes, and we ended up getting off at a stop in the historical district, and . . ."

She went on and on like this for the short remainder of the trip, hands clutching the book in her lap. Watching Constance with great interest, Penny was beginning to grasp another emotion.

Anxiety, tightening of your gutstrings, heightening your pitch, changing your tune.

Apparently, this emotion was contagious. Sometimes on *Storm at Dawn,* the background music would swell, the chords becoming more dissonant, indicating to the listener that something bad was about to happen that the characters were unaware of. Penny felt that way now. Particularly when the train pulled up to the station and she spotted a few security guards on the platform.

After retrieving their bags, Constance and Penny followed the Goldsteins off the train. Constance squeezed

Penny's hand tightly, and Penny felt an unspoken message in the gesture: *Stay close and do as I do.* Her heart—Chance's heart—responded with another *thump-thump.*

"It was very nice to meet you both," Constance said. "I hope you move to Daystar. I really think you'll love it there."

"Thank you, dear." Mrs. Goldstein glanced around the platform. "Where are your parents?"

"We're meeting them near the flower shop just outside of the main concourse," Constance replied immediately. "Have a lovely evening!" She tugged Penny's hand, but as soon as they started walking, Mrs. Goldstein fell into step beside them.

"We're heading that way as well," she said with a smile, then glanced over her shoulder at her husband. "Aren't we, dear?"

Mr. Goldstein grumbled something that sounded like "Apparently, we are now," then adopted a look of innocence when his wife narrowed her eyes.

Constance's smile remained fixed, but her grip on Penny's hand began to hurt. When they entered the main concourse, Penny did a quick scan of the few people milling about. She was hoping to spot an adult near the flower shop; maybe that would be enough to put Mrs. Goldstein's mind at rest. A group of teenagers were lounging in the chairs at the center of the concourse, a man in a suit was purchasing a ticket, and two women even older than the Goldsteins were chatting away on a bench near the exit.

Penny zeroed in on the man in the suit because he looked as though he could be her father—tall and graceful, with curly black hair, and skin just about the color of a walnut. Then she caught herself and shook her head. They needed to find an adult who could pass as a parent for Constance and Chance, not Penny.

For just a moment, though, she'd had that sense of familiarity again. As though the man in the suit really could have been her father. But marionettes didn't have fathers. Unless the puppeteer counted, because he created them. But how could he create something that had a soul? Penny gazed at the tall man. His suit was nice, but the pants ended a bit too high, and the jacket was perhaps a tad too tight.

I know what you aren't. *I want to know what you* are.

Suddenly, Penny became very aware that the body she currently inhabited was not her own. In just over a day, she had grown accustomed to walking and breathing and talking out loud. She had acclimated so quickly that it had been easy to pretend this was her body. But now, in this moment in a nearly deserted train station, Penny felt quite acutely the fact that she was wearing a suit that didn't fit. And when this adventure was over, she would have to return it. She would go back to living inside a girl-shaped shell that couldn't move or do anything at all.

It hardly seemed fair. Why should Chance's soul deserve a body that could jump and shout and dance, and her soul be trapped in a wooden cage?

Her *soul*. Penny dismissed the thought quickly, because Constance could not be right about that. Marionettes couldn't possibly have *souls*. Penny would not allow herself to even hope that such a ridiculous thing might be true. Because that might lead to *wanting* a soul. And Penny was not some demon puppet who stole souls from children.

Or bodies. This body did not belong to her, and she would return it because it was the right thing to do.

And for now she would not dwell on the fact that afterward she would be doomed to her wooden prison forever.

"No sign of your parents, looks like," Mrs. Goldstein was saying. "Should we perhaps—"

"It's okay, happens all the time!" Constance's voice came out in a squeak. "We live nearby, um, I mean we're *staying* nearby—we can walk." But the words hadn't even left her mouth when Mrs. Goldstein shook her head vehemently.

"Oh, absolutely not, it's the middle of the night!" She clucked her tongue and glanced at her watch, disapproval deepening the wrinkles around her eyes and mouth. "Honestly, children riding the trains alone in the day is one thing, but I can't . . ." She paused, pressing her lips together. "Well, that's none of my business. But I refuse to let you two walk around alone. It's out of the question."

Mr. Goldstein stifled a yawn. "There's a police officer over there," he croaked, gesturing over by the ticket booth.

His wife's face lit up. "Ah, perfect. Let's see if we can get you two a ride, okay?"

With that, she strode across the concourse, clearly expecting the others to follow. Mr. Goldstein covered his mouth with his arm to muffle another yawn as he trailed after her. Constance and Penny looked at one another.

"Have you ever run before?" Constance whispered.

Penny shook her head.

"Think you can?"

"Yes."

And without another word, the two sprinted off toward the exit, still gripping each other's hands tightly.

They weren't even halfway to the door when a voice that belonged to neither of the Goldsteins shouted something. But Penny couldn't hear it over the rush of blood in her ears, the sound of her own breathing suddenly amplified. She didn't look to see if the police officer was chasing them. She just focused on the EXIT sign and pumped her legs—Chance's legs—as fast as they would go.

Constance reached the doors a split second before Penny. She slammed into them without slowing her speed, and the two of them stumbled out onto the street. Penny barely had a chance to take in her surroundings before Constance yanked her arm, and they were off again. A few seconds later, Penny heard the doors burst open, followed by a shout. She did not look back.

This street was nothing like the one the Museum of the Peculiar Arts called home. Unfathomably high skyscrapers lined the avenue, blocking most of the night sky from view.

Despite the late hour, cars and buses still sat at every intersection as pedestrians, many dressed to the nines and laughing loudly, crossed the streets in a never-ending exchange from one restaurant or club to the next. Penny barely kept pace with Constance, who ran with purpose, as though she were heading toward something and not away.

Half a block ahead, a bus idled at its stop. It let out a huge hiss of exhaust and pulled away from the curb, and Constance shouted, *"Wait!"* She put on an extra burst of speed, still dragging Penny behind her, and pounded on the side of the bus with her free hand. The bus jerked to a halt, and Constance hurtled up the steps. Ignoring the bus driver's irritated stare, she pulled out her coin purse and dumped a fistful of coins into the slot before pulling Penny to a pair of empty seats in the very back. Panting heavily, Penny stared out the back window as the bus pulled into the street. The police officer was peering into the window of a restaurant, frowning.

Constance and Penny slumped down in their seats and looked at one another. Then Constance started to giggle.

Penny didn't understand why, because what had just happened was not at all funny. But for some reason, laughter bubbled up in her own throat in response. And then the two were doubled over in hysterics, shoulders shaking, tears streaming down their faces.

Penny felt Chance's heart thumping a gradually slowing *boom, boom, boom* against his rib cage; she felt the rawness in his throat; she felt the way his bones suddenly seemed lighter, the way the muscles in his calves ached, how his legs wobbled in a way that assured her that standing was not an option at the moment.

It felt *wonderful*.

"Well," Constance said at last, her cheeks flushed and her eyes bright. "That was fun."

"Fun?" Penny repeated it as a question, because even though she agreed, she couldn't figure out why. "If that officer had caught us, we might never find Chance. It was frightening."

Constance smiled. "It was *thrilling*," she corrected Penny. "Like *Storm at Dawn*. You can't have an adventure without a little risk." Leaning past Penny, she squinted out the window and sighed. "We're heading uptown."

"Is that bad?"

"Kind of," Constance said. "The park is just south of here. But the carnival will be all closed up at this time anyway. We need to find a place to hide for the night, and then we can head to the park in the morning."

"Where will we hide?"

Closing her eyes, Constance took a few deep breaths. A smile still lingered around her lips.

"I don't know. That's what makes this an adventure."

SPINNING

Just before sunrise, the puppeteer sat down behind the spinning wheel. The darkness behind him seemed to expand, like the cabinet was taking a deep yawn.

Chance watched from his spot in the cupboard. He waited. But the puppeteer stayed perfectly still.

The spinning wheel was driving Chance slightly mad. He saw it even when the door was closed, as if it were etched into his glass eyes. Perhaps it was easier to fixate on the wheel than on his situation, which seemed more and more hopeless with every passing minute. Chance could not focus on that, because there was nothing to be done about it. He could not think about Fortunato's betrayal without falling into what the Storm would call "the endless gray abyss of despair."

Instead, he spent his time pondering the spinning wheel and what the puppeteer might do with it.

So far, he'd just spun and watched the spokes fly, his expression contemplative.

Right now, though, the puppeteer's mouth was contorted in a grimace. A feverish glint lit up his eyes as he spun the wheel faster and faster. His fingers and hands and arms moved stiffly, as if he were a tin man whose joints needed oiling. He bared his teeth in frustration, and Chance suddenly wished he could stop watching, because now the puppeteer looked less like a man and more like a monster.

Then, with a sharp hissing sound, the puppeteer stood abruptly, hands trembling at his sides.

"Not even a little bit?" he hissed. "Surely there must be *something* left."

He glared down at the spinning wheel as if it had done him personal harm. Then he left the cabinet and slammed the door. He crossed the trailer, opened another cabinet, and after a few seconds of rummaging around, pulled out a small knife and a hand mirror.

A wave of foreboding washed over Chance as the

puppeteer examined his reflection. The man angled his face to study the gnarled wart on his neck. Then he lifted the knife and, in a quick, violent gesture, hacked the lump of skin off with a look of grim satisfaction.

Chance screamed silently, focusing his gaze on the cabinet that contained the spinning wheel. After several seconds, he looked back at the puppeteer, bracing himself for a bloody, gaping wound.

But, impossibly, the puppeteer's neck was clean.

No blood, not even a scratch. His skin was still as colorless as ever. The puppeteer studied what Chance assumed was the wart in his cupped hand. Then he set it heavily on the table with a soft plunk. Chance stared at the shiny, hardened thing and was reminded forcibly of the base of the spindle. The memory of the weight of it in his palm, warm and glowing with magic, put thoughts in Chance's head that he did not wish to ponder further.

Calmer now, the puppeteer put the knife back in its drawer. Then he glanced over at Chance. Slowly he walked over to the cupboard. He did not speak or smile. In fact, Chance had the distinct impression he was allowing Chance to take a closer look, to confirm what he'd just witnessed. And there, on the puppeteer's neck, was a small indent where the wart had been. It looked as though someone had shaved a shallow chunk out of a bar of soap.

The puppeteer smiled, as if he'd heard the thought and agreed.

Then he went back into the cabinet with the spinning wheel and closed the door, leaving Chance with nothing but questions, violent images, and no hope of even sleep as an escape.

LOST SOUL

An early sunbeam shone through the stained-glass window of a church on 145th Street, casting a colorful kaleidoscope over the pale faces of the two children in the first pew. The girl slept with a gentle smile on her face, as if her dreams were filled with rainbows and sunshine. The boy curled up at her side slept more fitfully. His brows were pulled together, and he was mumbling incoherently.

Sister Maria Ignacia was the first to arrive for morning prayer, and therefore the one to discover the two children. For a few minutes she fretted over what to do, reluctant to leave them alone long enough for her to call someone to help. Yet she feared that they would panic when they saw her upon waking and would flee.

At last she sat very quietly at the boy's side to wait for the others to arrive for service. She wondered when the two had turned up. The church had had midnight Mass last night, but only about a dozen had attended, and Sister Maria Ignacia was sure she had not seen these two faces among them. They must have entered the church after one in the morning, a distressing thought given their ages and the fact that they were quite without adult supervision.

This, truth be told, was another reason Sister Maria Ignacia was hesitant to call for help. Because if these children were runaways, the police would take them home. But Sister Maria Ignacia knew from experience that children who risked sneaking out of their homes in the dead of night often had very good reasons.

On the other hand, the city held potentially greater threats. Last month the orphanage at which Sister Maria Ignacia volunteered on weekends had reported a missing boy. And back in the spring, posters had gone up for twins who had run away from home, leaving their grandparents distraught. The nun had kept these children in her prayers, their names a mantra in her mind: *Linda Goldstein, Lyle Goldstein, Jack Wright*. She knew many had given up hope.

She could never do that, though. She believed they might still be found.

And Gil, too. He'd vanished months ago, and his family feared the worst, but she refused to give up on her sweet young nephew.

Linda Goldstein. Lyle Goldstein. Jack Wright. Gil Espinosa.

Sister Maria Ignacia normally loved summer. The warmth, the sunshine that persisted into late evening, the geraniums that bloomed from patches of grass here and there along the paved sidewalks. And the carnival, always a sea of smiles and bright, sunburned faces. Gil had adored the carnival. He'd talked about it all spring, right up until the day he disappeared.

This summer was different. As if some invisible shadow loomed over the city, darkening its soul. The very air felt charged, full of static, ready to burn at any moment. Sister Maria Ignacia had found herself returning to the convent well before dark and avoiding the park altogether. She knew, logically, that this must be because of what had happened to Gil. Her nephew's disappearance had threatened to destroy her entire family. Paranoia had caused her brother and his wife to all but lock their remaining children in their rooms to keep them safe. They went to school, they went to church, they went home. And while Sister Maria Ignacia believed deeply in the power of prayer, she could tell her brother's children were frustrated with their parents' passivity and their own confinement. They longed to take action. To search every corner of the city until they found Gil and brought him home.

Sister Maria Ignacia empathized. But like her brother and his wife, she could not bear the thought of losing another precious child. They could not take that risk.

"Mmphf."

Startled, Sister Maria Ignacia looked down at the boy. His eyelashes were fluttering now, exposing the whites of his eyes in flashes. She fought the urge to offer a comforting hand, worried she would wake him. If the children panicked upon seeing her and ran off, she could do nothing to stop them. And she wanted to help.

The boy whimpered, and her heart ached for him. His mumblings grew louder, his fingers and feet twitching, and then his eyes flew open and he cried:

"Lottie!"

"It's okay," Sister Maria Ignacia said in the most soothing voice she could manage. Which was difficult, because the boy's expression was genuinely alarming. His mouth was stretched in a silent scream, his blue-green eyes darting rapidly from the altar to the stained-glass window to Sister Maria Ignacia's face to his own hands, upon which his gaze settled. The nun, more than a little disturbed and hesitant to frighten him further, watched as he wiggled the pinkie on his right hand, and then the forefinger and thumb on his left. He stared back up at Sister Maria Ignacia, and a thought entered her mind as clearly as if someone had whispered it in her ear.

This is a lost soul.

Her eyes welled with tears, which she blinked back. "You're safe here," she said quietly. "I promise."

The boy's sister stretched and yawned, and when her sleepy eyes focused on the nun, she leaped to her feet as if she'd been shocked.

"Oh! Good morning!" she cried, smoothing out her skirt and tucking her hair behind her ears. "We came in extra early to, um, say a few prayers before breakfast, and—"

"You spent the night," Sister Maria Ignacia said gently, charmed by the girl's flustered manner. "It's okay. You're both welcome here."

"Oh, well, thank you, I'm sorry," the girl babbled as she tugged her brother's arm. "Come on, Chance, we need to get home. Mom's probably wondering what's taking us so long."

"Please, wait." Sister Maria Ignacia got to her feet as well. She stole another glance at the boy, who seemed to have mostly collected himself, though his eyes were still a bit wild. "If you're in trouble, I can help you."

"No, everything's fine!" the girl exclaimed. "We're just late, that's all. Chance, let's go."

Sister Maria Ignacia watched helplessly as the two scurried down the aisle. She took a step after them and then stopped, for what could she do to keep them here? Nothing.

But there was something else she could do. She didn't want to, she wasn't sure it was *right,* but it was her duty.

Once the doors had closed behind them, the nun walked past the altar and slipped through the exit. At the end of a short hallway, she opened the empty classroom in which she taught Sunday school, picked up the phone on the desk, and dialed the police station.

NOT DÉJÀ VU

Penny and Constance did not speak as they left the church. Constance kept a firm grip on Penny's hand but did not run, though Penny suspected she was fighting the urge. Instead, they walked briskly around the corner, down a block, a right turn, two more blocks, and a left turn, then finally slowed their pace.

"I shouldn't have said his name," Constance said. Her eyes were closed, and she was drawing deep, shaky breaths.

"What?"

"I called you Chance in front of that nun. *Twice.*"

Shaking her head, Constance shifted her bag from one shoulder to the other. "If she calls the police and gives them one of our names, and my parents have reported us missing, they'll know we were here."

"Then, we just have to keep moving," Penny told her, and they did.

Constance gave Penny one of the sandwiches they'd packed, then took the other for herself. She thought out loud as they ate and walked.

"I still have some money left, but not much. It's a long walk to the park, but I'd rather save the bus fare, because we're going to need more food eventually. Oh, that nun was nice, I feel awful for being so rude and running out of there, but there's no way she would have believed us, you know? About Chance, I mean. I can't imagine what she would have said if we'd told her the truth about you."

That I'm a demon? Probably not welcome in a church. Penny did not think this was what Constance meant, which was why she kept the thought to herself. Still, something about the way Constance said it stung a little bit.

As Constance rambled on, Penny remained silent and focused on the dream she'd had. Or at least she tried to. But the moment Penny had opened her eyes, the details had begun leaking out like water through a sieve. The emotions had lingered, though. Very strong emotions. Fear, confusion, anger. And another one, a powerful emotion Penny didn't have a word for, but just the memory of it filled her

138

to bursting, made her feel as though she'd do anything for it. It was a beautiful, terrifying feeling, like soaring uncontrollably across the sky with no hope of stopping, and no desire to.

She wondered if the content of the dream, whatever images had filled it, had come from her or Chance. It was, after all, still Chance's brain in this body. Perhaps it had accessed his memories while his body slept.

"You lost, little lady?"

Penny blinked, shaking these thoughts from her mind. A man was slumped on a bench outside a barbershop with a CLOSED sign in the window. He was looking at Constance. Penny looked at Constance too.

She smiled. "No, sir, we're fine."

"Sure I can't help you with anything?"

Penny was confused. The man's words seemed kind, but something was off. The corners of his mouth had curved up, but it wasn't a smile, exactly. And his eyes slid up and down Constance as if she were an item he was considering for purchase.

"No," Constance chirped. "We're meeting our father right up the street. He's taking us to the carnival for the day. He's driving, and our car is parked right around the corner, so . . ."

Constance, Penny was beginning to learn, spoke even faster when she lied.

"Clear now, but it's supposed to rain this afternoon,"

the man said, gesturing at the silvery sky. "Don't want to get that pretty hair wet. I've got an umbrella here." He patted the black umbrella Penny now saw lying beside him on the bench.

"I'm sure our father will have one," Constance said. Her voice was still cheery, but it was hard underneath, like a layer of silk over steel.

"You sure? I don't mind walking you over there."

"That's all right," Constance said firmly, squeezing Penny's arm until she winced. The man still had not given Penny so much as a glance, as though she were invisible. They began to walk again, and the man called out:

"Come on now, honey. Don't I at least get a 'thank you'?"

Penny's heart was pounding hard now, like when she'd run away from the police officer. She heard Constance let out the softest of sighs before facing the man again.

"Thank you, sir!" And before he could respond, she set off down the street, pulling Penny along. Penny glanced over her shoulder at the man, whose eyes still lingered on Constance.

They turned the next corner, and Constance let go of Penny's arm. She kept walking, the same fixed smile on her face. But Penny noticed her hands shaking a bit.

"It's fine," Constance said, blinking rapidly. "We'll be fine. We just need to get to the park."

Penny suspected that Constance was actually talking

to herself, so she didn't answer. She wasn't sure what to say anyway. The entire encounter had been very confusing, and she couldn't figure out why, exactly, she felt this unsettled by it.

They walked another block in silence. Penny was still thinking about the Thank-You Man, and several minutes passed without her taking in her surroundings. But when she saw the market on the corner, she stopped in her tracks.

"What's wrong?" Constance asked, frowning.

Penny exhaled slowly. She wanted to explain this just right.

"I have this feeling," she told Constance, her eyes still locked on the market. "I've had it a few times since Chance and I swapped, but it's really strong right now, and I don't know the word for it. That market down there, with the yellow awning? It feels . . . familiar. Like I've been there. But I've never even seen it before, so that doesn't make sense."

Constance's face relaxed into a real smile. "Oh, that's déjà vu!"

"What?"

"Déjà vu," she explained. "It's when you feel like you've experienced something before even when you haven't."

"Do you ever feel that way?"

"Sure!" Constance shrugged. "Sometimes. Happens to everyone occasionally."

Penny wondered if it ever happened to anyone several times in less than two days. The chores, the lanky man at the train station in the ill-fitting suit, the song that had played on the radio in the car. At least she had an explanation now, and a word to match the emotion.

"Have you and Chance ever been to this neighborhood?" Penny asked.

Constance shook her head. "My mother says it's 'shady.' Really she just means it's old, you know? It hasn't gone all modern like our neighborhood. But I'm not lost, if that's what you're worried about. If we keep walking south, we'll hit the north end of the park eventually."

Penny was not worried about being lost. She was wondering if this déjà vu could be attributed to Chance's having been here before. And perhaps he had. Penny would not be surprised if Chance had visited this neighborhood without his mother's permission. It seemed like a very Chance thing to do.

They passed the market, and the feeling grew stronger. Penny actually began to wonder if she had the power of premonition, like the Storm—it was as if she could predict what she would see next. A small bank across the street. A patio with chipped blue paint and potted sunflowers. A five-and-dime store next to a firehouse.

No sooner did she imagine each of these things than her eyes found them. They stood out among the other businesses and brownstones. They were different.

They were *older.*

This was not déjà vu. Penny knew it was impossible, but

she felt certain she'd seen this neighborhood before, she'd *been* here before. She said nothing to Constance, just picked up her pace. Without thinking about it, Penny began to lead instead of follow.

"No, we need to go this way," Constance said when Penny turned sharply at the next corner. "Wait, where are you going?"

"I don't know!" Penny cried, which was the truth. And yet she had a destination in mind. With each step, the image became just a little bit clearer. It was like a word on the tip of her tongue, just seconds away from fully forming.

At the sight of a furniture store across the intersection, Penny broke into a run. She might as well have still had her strings; the pull she felt was physical. It was just up ahead, this place she couldn't quite name; it would be sandwiched between the furniture store and a café, a squat brick building painted blue with swirls of white like clouds, and a silver awning with fancy script:

Club Heavenly Blues.

Penny came to an abrupt halt, gazing at the jazz club across the street. She'd never seen it before, but every detail was achingly familiar. Her breath came in shallow gasps, and her heart hammered in her chest. She had to go inside. There were answers in that club, answers to questions she'd never asked, and darned if that didn't make any sense at all, but if she could just—

"Penny?"

Constance touched her arm, jolting Penny from her thoughts.

"I know this place, Lottie," she whispered.

A beat passed, then another. The two girls looked at one another.

"Constance," Penny corrected herself. "Sorry, I—I meant Constance."

She did not know where *Lottie* had come from. But she remembered, very suddenly, that she had yelled that name when she awoke in the church pew.

And here it was again, that feeling of having experienced something before. Only now it really was déjà vu. Because Penny had witnessed this before—someone else in distress, crying out a name that was not the *right* name, a name that had been plucked from some locked-away part of his soul in a moment of panic.

She heard, in her head, Fortunato crying out *"Nicolette!"* as Penny had tumbled off her shelf.

She had no idea what any of this could mean. Her brain was connecting dots, but the dots were failing to form a complete picture.

Thankfully, Constance did not ask Penny to share her thoughts. Instead, she squinted at the building across the street.

"Isn't this the club with the live music that comes on after *Storm at Dawn*?"

Penny nodded. "Yes. It's my favorite radio program. But

I—I knew it would be here. Because of the déjà vu. But I don't think it's déjà vu. I just . . . I have to go inside. Just for a second."

She glanced up and down the street, then hurried across. All sorts of emotions were roiling around inside her now, just like they had in her dream. What would she find inside?

Or *whom*?

Eagerly Penny grasped the doors and tugged. They didn't budge.

"Closed," Constance said softly behind her. Looking down, Penny saw the sign taped to the glass door: OPEN SEVEN DAYS A WEEK, 6 P.M. TO 4 A.M. Her eyes started to burn, and she pressed her face to the door, straining to see something, anything. But the darkness was absolute.

A tear trickled down Penny's cheek. Her vision blurred. She took a step back, overwhelmed and exhausted and wanting nothing more than to curl up into a ball on the sidewalk and sleep. Something soft touched her cheek, and Penny blinked rapidly.

Gently Constance wiped her tears away with a handkerchief. "You cried in the car, too," she said. "When that song came on."

Penny swallowed. "I know. But I don't know why."

"Hmm." Constance folded the handkerchief and began tucking it back into her bag. "Do you remember anything from before the museum?"

145

"No." Penny closed her eyes, picturing the dusty shelves and glass cases. "I know I've forgotten things. Because all I remember is being on the shelf, and a little bit about a stage, and someone holding my strings, but—what's wrong?"

Constance, who had been rummaging around the inside of her bag, knelt down and dumped its contents onto the ground. Penny watched as she separated the items: a dress, socks, underwear, shoes, book, bananas. Then, with a deep sigh, Constance looked up at her.

"My coin purse is gone," she said. "It must have fallen out in the church."

They were silent for a moment, absorbing the full impact. No money meant no food, no transportation, and most devastatingly, no carnival tickets. They could go back to the church, but then they would risk running into the nun, who might have called the police.

"We can't go back there," Constance decided. "We can't risk getting caught, because then we'll never find Chance."

"But we'll never find Chance if we can't get into the carnival," Penny pointed out.

"We need to keep heading for the park, and . . ."

A shadow fell over the two before Constance could finish. They both looked up into the frowning faces of two police officers, and suddenly the park seemed as distant as the moon.

THE SOUL INSIDE THE PRINCESS

The Princess Penny Puppet Show made its debut at ten o'clock.

While the puppeteer had had different marionettes in the past, the story in his show remained the same. It began with a slightly scratchy trumpet fanfare piping through the speakers hidden under the stage. The children, bright-eyed with anticipation, quieted immediately and settled on the grass. Behind them, the adults smiled uneasily at one another, each overcome with nostalgia and a vague sense of wariness they didn't quite understand.

The curtain rose, and the children, most of whom had never seen one of the puppeteer's lifelike, life-size marionettes up close, gasped in awe at the sight of Princess Penny. Her curly black hair hung in a thick braid over one shoulder, a tiara gleaming on top of her head. Her dress was lavender silk with white lace trim, and she clutched a tiny bouquet of daisies, which mostly hid her mangled fingers. A beam of sunlight hit her face like a spotlight, drawing a golden hue from the dark brown wood and making her eyes sparkle and dance. The screen behind her featured a painted field of flowers and served to hide the platform where the puppeteer stood, holding her strings.

For a moment, Princess Penny hung in dignified silence as the fanfare finished.

Then a tinkly waltz began to play, and the princess sang:

"What a pretty day! What a pretty day! What a pretty day-y-y!"

The children shrieked with laughter. The puppeteer was, of course, providing Penny's voice, and it was high and shrill. The lyrics, too, were almost self-mocking in their simplicity as the princess explained that all she wanted to do every day was pick flowers. She skipped and spun in circles in front of the painted screen, which slowly moved to the side, giving the effect that she was dancing through the field. When the Sheepherder appeared, the children cheered and clapped.

Like Princess Penny, this marionette was extraordinarily

realistic. His hair was black and wavy, and his dark eyes seemed to be lit from within. He was made from cherry wood a much lighter shade of brown than Penny's. He wore a cinnamon-colored robe and carried a staff, and the cotton-ball sheep at his side drew "awws" from the younger children in the audience.

Princess Penny and the Sheepherder sang a duet together, during which he explained to her how fulfilling it was to herd sheep. The puppeteer gave him a mild voice, almost dignified in comparison with the princess's silly squeak. They frolicked off the stage as the happy melody came to an end. The applause quickly turned to "oohs" and "aahs" as the screen rotated to reveal a dungeon background.

The Evil Witch dropped down suddenly, and the children screamed in delight and fear. This marionette was painted green, but she was otherwise just as lifelike as the first two had been. Her eyes were bright blue, and though her face was smooth and youthful, she wore a frizzy gray wig. The music turned ominous as she flew back and forth across the stage on her broom, then fretted over her cauldron, cooking up a plan to capture the princess and singing her spells in a crackly, cackly voice.

Once the audience was informed of the Evil Witch's plan, the scene shifted back to the field. Princess Penny came across a bottle of green liquid in the flowers and, despite warnings from the Sheepherder and shouts of despair from the children, decided there would be no harm in trying a sip. She instantly fell into a deep sleep, and the Sheepherder sang a song of regret and gentle admonishment.

The screen rotated again, and now the Brave Knight took the stage to loud cheers. He declared in a rousing chant that he would rescue the princess with sinew and steel—but first he would have to consult the wisest man in the land for advice.

In a poof of smoke, the Wise Wizard appeared. His eyes were the same bright blue as the Evil Witch's, and a long white wig and fake beard obscured most of his face.

Through song the Wise Wizard informed the Brave Knight about the Evil Witch's one weakness: sunlight. She remained in her dungeon, brewing potions and casting spells to carry out her nefarious plans for the kingdom. The only way to defeat her was to draw her outside of her dungeon into the light. But even getting into her dungeon would be next to impossible, as it was guarded by a fearsome dragon.

For the Brave Knight, a dragon posed no threat. He charged into the cave that served as an entrance to the witch's dungeon, sword drawn. A spark of flames and a distant roar just offstage caused the children to gasp. But their whimpers quickly turned to giggles when the dragon bobbed into view. Even the scariest of creatures didn't seem frightening at all when they were made from twisted balloons.

The battle was brief, and soon the Brave Knight's sword

found its mark, destroying the dragon with a loud *POP* that elicited more screams from the giddy audience. He soon found Princess Penny locked in a tower, and upon seeing one another for the first time, they sang a song of true love. The Brave Knight freed the princess, and they fled the tower, seemingly unaware that the Evil Witch was watching them go.

But thanks to the Wise Wizard, the Brave Knight had planned for this in secret. He stopped just outside the cave, taunting the Evil Witch, who of course could not step out into the sunlight. "You fool!" she cackled, for her powers extended everywhere, and there was no escape for the princess. But then the Sheepherder, who had been hiding behind a rock, leaped out behind the Evil Witch and pushed her out of the cave! She screeched horribly as steam rose around her, and then she collapsed and vanished, dropping into a trapdoor beneath the stage.

Princess Penny sang her gratitude for the Brave Knight, the Sheepherder, and the Wise Wizard. Then she danced one last time through the field of flowers, and the curtain began to lower. The children clapped and cried for more. They did not want the show to end.

Neither did the soul inside the princess.

He did not want the adoring audience to disappear behind that curtain. He wanted to keep dancing on the stage forever. It made him feel alive again. He could almost convince himself he was really breathing and moving. Not like when he was in the cupboard in the trailer, with nothing to do but look and think and let the mind fog dull his emotions and swallow his memories one by one.

The fog kept trying to take his name. He kept that important piece of himself tucked into the safest corner of his mind and guarded it as best he could. This wasn't the kind of adventure he had wanted, paralyzed and powerless, fighting off an invisible demon hell-bent on stealing his very identity. With every passing minute, it seemed easier to just let it happen. Maybe he used to be a real, living boy, but not anymore.

Now he was just a marionette.

A FAMILIAR STRANGER

Inside the local police station a few blocks west of Club Heavenly Blues, three children sat on a bench in the hallway. The receptionist had been asked to keep an eye on them, which was proving to be an easy task. On the left, a white girl with a remarkably cheery disposition given her surroundings sat lost in thoughts that caused her mouth to smile but her eyes to flash like steel. Next to her was a boy who was clearly her brother, fidgeting and shifting like his skeleton wanted to shake loose of his skin. And on the far right, a little separate from those two, was a tall black boy of about fourteen who stared at his hands, which were clasped in his lap as if in prayer.

"Constance and Chance Bonvillain?"

All three heads snapped up as the police chief stepped out of his office. Constance's smile broadened.

"Yes, sir?"

The man's face softened a bit. "I've spoken with your parents, hon, and they're on their way. Gave them quite a fright, you two. Running off like that."

Constance's expression was contrite. "I know, sir. We're sorry, sir. We just moved out to Daystar Meadows, you see, and my brother insisted on coming back to say goodbye to a friend of ours, and we ended up getting lost, and—"

The police chief raised his hand. "You've told me, yes. We'll all sit down when your parents get here and talk this through. As for you," he added, turning to the tall boy on the right side of the bench. "This is strike three, son. Mrs. Pepperton will be here in a few minutes."

The boy drew a deep breath before lifting his eyes. "It's my brother, sir. He's been missing for over a month now, and I just—"

"You just thought you'd run off to find him yourself?" The chief's face held no kindness now. "Howard, believe me, we've been looking for Jack. But he's not the only child who's run off. And you aren't doing Mrs. Pepperton any favors by doing the same. That's what got Jack in trouble in the first—"

"My brother didn't run away," Howard interrupted. He didn't raise his voice at all, but anger radiated off him. The police chief waved a dismissive hand and returned to his office, muttering under his breath.

The three children sat in silence for a long minute. Penny kept stealing sidelong glances at Howard. Perhaps this déjà vu thing was truly driving her mad, but even this boy seemed familiar. Not his face, specifically. Just . . . something about him.

Howard noticed Penny staring and shifted uncomfortably in his seat. At last Constance turned to him.

"You're looking for your brother?"

Howard swallowed. "Yes. He disappeared last month."

"I'm very sorry. My brother . . ." Pausing, Constance pressed her lips together. "So you ran away to look for him? What about your parents—aren't they looking too?"

"My parents are dead." Howard stared down at his clasped hands again. "We live at Mrs. Pepperton's—she runs an orphanage on One Hundred Tenth Street. And I know the police think that's why Jack ran away. But he'd never run off without me. We're family—we don't have anyone else. I don't know what happened to him. He just disappeared one day. No one saw anything suspicious; it was like he just . . . he was gone. Like magic."

Howard spoke slowly, and every word sank into Penny's mind like heavy rocks tossed into a pond. She sat up slowly, her eyes fixed on Howard's face.

"I have to find him," Howard told his hands. His voice

quivered. "I have to. And I can't do that just sitting around at Mrs. Pepperton's."

"Of course you can't," Constance agreed. "We need to leave, right now. All of us."

Howard blinked at her. "What?"

"My brother is missing too," Constance told him. "But my parents will never believe me. We have to leave before they get here."

"Isn't that your brother?" Howard pointed at Penny.

"No. It's a long story." Constance peered up and down the hall. At one end was a door marked EXIT, with a sign beneath that read EMERGENCY ONLY: ALARM WILL SOUND. At the other end was the lobby, where the watchful receptionist monitored everyone who came and went.

"We need a distraction," Penny said. She still felt a lingering drowsiness from the strange events of the last few hours: the dream she'd had in the church, finding Club Heavenly Blues, and now this boy, Howard, a familiar stranger. But there was no time to dwell on those feelings, much as she wanted to explore them. Their current situation was dire, and they needed to escape.

Thanks to *Storm at Dawn,* Penny knew exactly how they were going to do it.

• • •

Not more than five minutes later, alarms began to wail. All along the hall, curious heads poked out of their doorways.

The police chief hurried out of his office. His eyes flickered from the empty bench over to the door marked EXIT, which was slowly closing. He ran down the hall and burst outside, shading his eyes from the bright silver sky and glancing around. The alley was empty.

The alarm stopped wailing when the police chief walked back inside and closed the door. He marched down the hall to the lobby, where the receptionist was still on her feet.

"They can't have gotten far," he told her. "If Mrs. Pepperton or the Bonvillains get here, don't tell them anything. Just let them know I'll be back soon."

The bells over the door jingled as he left.

The receptionist sat back down at her desk and resumed filing, and the others returned to their offices. Nearly five minutes had passed when the receptionist heard a child's whisper.

"Shh! They'll hear you!"

Frowning, the receptionist stood slowly and crept down the hallway. She could hear the muffled sounds of phone calls and typing coming from behind each door. At the restroom, she stopped and listened hard.

The sink was running.

Chewing her lip, the receptionist wondered if she should get someone to help her. Then she dismissed the thought. They were just children. Standing up straighter, she pushed the door open.

"Okay, you three. Time to . . ."

The restroom was empty.

The receptionist checked all three stalls just to be sure. When she stepped back into the hall, her eyes narrowed.

The police chief's door, which had most definitely been closed, was now ajar.

Irritated, she crossed the hall and pushed the door open with more force than perhaps was necessary. "Enough of this. I need you kids to . . ."

The office was empty too.

The receptionist's confusion lasted only another second, until she heard the faint sound of bells jingling. She ran down the hall and into the lobby, which was empty. Anxiety knotted her stomach as she hurried to the door and peered up and down the street.

No sign of the children. Maybe she'd been mistaken.

There was no need to tell the police chief about this, she decided. He was already out there looking for them. And really, her ears had probably been playing tricks on her. She shook her head, decided she was not to blame for any of this, and headed back to her desk.

Across the street, three children huddled behind a parked car until the door closed. Then they sprinted down the street as fast as their legs would carry them.

THE BRAVE KNIGHT

The puppeteer was in a foul mood.

The marionette—no, Chance, his name was Chance; the fog had not taken that yet—watched from the cupboard as the puppeteer sewed a tear in the Evil Witch's black dress, which had caught on a nail in the stage during the previous performance. It took the puppeteer nearly a full minute just to thread the needle, as he kept stopping to flex and crack his stiff fingers.

Now that the show was over, now that he was back in the trailer, Chance remembered his situation. He supposed he should be alarmed by what had happened to him during the performance. The moment the curtain had risen, he'd forgotten what it was to be anyone but Princess Penny. The only thing that had kept him from losing himself entirely in the story was the shrill falsetto the puppeteer had provided him. It had been nothing like Penny's real voice, which was soft and low. And *that* had reminded Chance that he was not Princess Penny at all, that the real Penny was out there somewhere in his body, with his family.

His family. Chance could picture them. But he couldn't quite recall what their voices sounded like.

Which, again, probably should have alarmed him. It would have if the fog weren't stealing his emotions, too. It was nice, actually, not to be bothered with the pesky business of feeling.

All Chance really wanted was another show, another performance.

A roar of anger jarred him from his thoughts. The puppeteer was staring at his hands, and at first Chance couldn't see anything wrong with them. Then he realized the puppeteer was straining, his teeth gritted with effort, veins pushing up against the skin of his arms. He was trying to curl his fingers into fists, but they remained as unbendable as twigs, and Chance was hit with the sudden mental image of each of them snapping in two.

Exhaling loudly, the puppeteer dropped his arms to his sides and closed his eyes. Then he picked up the Evil Witch and brought her over to the cabinet. Chance flinched as the puppeteer shoved the Brave Knight over to make room for the witch. He scowled at each of his marionettes in turn, as if they'd done him personal harm. Then he slammed the cabinet door closed.

Chance felt something slump against his shoulder and realized the knight had fallen to the side. He wondered what was wrong with the puppeteer's hands. And then a voice that was not his own responded:

I think he's sick.

It was just like the first time Penny spoke to him when he'd touched her strings, Chance remembered with a jolt. And then the same voice said:

Hello? Can . . . can you hear me?

It was a boy's voice, quiet and shy, but excited.

Yes, I can, Chance thought back. *Are you the Brave Knight?*

Yes. Are you Princess Penny?

Yes, Chance replied, the thrill of his first conversation in ages zipping through him. *Our strings must be touching. That's how marionettes talk.*

You sound like a boy, the knight thought.

I am, Chance told him. *I accidentally swapped bodies with the real Penny. My name is Chance.*

You swapped? The knight sounded confused. *How?* And then Chance explained the whole story, which didn't take very long, as he could think much faster than he could talk. As he did, more details rushed back to him, so quickly and with such clarity that Chance was astounded he'd managed to forget them at all. He finished with learning about Fortunato's betrayal.

That's terrible, the knight said. *I'm sorry.*

Thank you. What's your name?

Just the Brave Knight. That's all the puppeteer ever called me.

This struck Chance as very sad. *How long have you been with him? How many shows have you done?*

There was a brief silence, but Chance could sense the knight's thoughts. They were murky and dense, like a swamp. *I don't know. I don't remember doing any other shows. All I really remember is being in the cabinet with the spinning wheel for a long time, in the dark.*

Heaviness settled over Chance. Why did the puppeteer create these magical marionettes with souls, doomed to a life on the shelf . . . or worse, in a box? It wasn't fair. *When Penny and I swap back, I'll take you both away from the puppeteer,* he told the knight emphatically. *The others, too. You'll never get locked up in the dark again.*

When you swap back? The knight sounded surprised. *How will you do that? You can't move or do anything. You're a damsel in distress, like in the show. All you can do is wait for someone to rescue you.*

Chance considered this. It was true that he couldn't move. But that didn't mean he couldn't do anything.

I have an idea, he told the knight, and the knight listened carefully.

MISSING

Penny, Constance, and Howard reached the north end of the park by noon. They would have reached it much faster had they not had to duck behind a tree or around a corner at the sight of anyone who resembled a police officer. The carnival took up the south end of the park, which was still a good two miles away. But rather than taking them into the park to cut through it, Constance led them around to walk the length along the west side.

"We don't have any money for tickets," she said. "We're going to the museum first, to see if Fortunato can help us."

"The museum closed," Penny reminded her. "He won't be there."

"He lives on the floor above it, though," Constance said. "We have to hope he's still there." She paused, turning to Penny. "We need him, Penny. We can't face this villain alone."

Penny nodded. Constance was right, of course. The man with the sharp face had given Chance the spindle that had swapped them. They had no idea why he'd done it, or what else he was capable of.

On Constance's other side, Howard cleared his throat. "Penny? I thought your name was Chance."

Constance and Penny exchanged a look. Then Constance smiled at Howard. "We've got a long walk ahead of us, so I guess we can tell you the whole story. Although you probably won't believe it."

Howard smiled back, and it was the first time since they'd met that he'd done so. His eyes softened, and Penny thought she saw the hint of a blush on his cheeks. "Try me," he said.

And so Constance launched into the tale as they walked. Her words drifted in and out of Penny's consciousness; she was too distracted by taking in the sights of the city, now that they weren't running for their lives. Constance took lots of turns and stuck to busier streets, which Penny suspected was deliberate. If they happened to be spotted by a police officer on the lookout for three reported runaways, it would be easier to disappear into a crowd. They walked through the theater district, where buildings loomed high overhead and lights in all colors flashed and blinked. Large posters featuring the titles of shows and the faces of their stars hung outside the theaters, and Penny couldn't help but wonder what it would be like to see such a performance. She even saw an advertisement for STORM AT DAWN, WITH A. P. HALLS. There was no photo, just a silhouette of a man in a trench coat and hat. Penny knew the Storm was a fictional character, but still, seeing the actor's name jarred her.

They passed the outskirts of the historical district, where a stately library sat filled with countless books Penny would never get to read. There were restaurants with menus outside highlighting all sorts of strange-sounding foods that Penny would never get to eat, and museums filled with paintings and sculptures Penny would never get to see. Because she was a marionette, not a person.

Envy, that black hole that swallows your heart and leaves you with an empty space that nothing can fill.

Penny suddenly became aware that Constance had stopped talking, and Howard was now staring at her. He looked away quickly, but not before Penny saw the fear in his eyes.

"So you . . . you're a . . ." Howard's throat moved visibly when he swallowed. "I don't understand."

"She's a marionette," Constance explained. "With a soul. Which she swapped with my brother's by accident."

Howard pressed his lips together. "It sounds a little bit like that old story, the one about these demon puppets who steal—"

"The Cabinetmaker's Apprentice!" cried Constance in delight, just as Penny said loudly: "I am not a demon!"

"I didn't say you were!" Howard sounded flustered. "It's just . . . what *are* you?"

He didn't say it unkindly, but Penny flinched.

"She is someone who needs help," Constance said before Penny could answer. "Like my brother. And your brother," she added. "You're an older sibling too, Howard. Right? So you understand."

She put a protective arm around Penny. Warmth spread through Penny from head to toe, and her envy subsided for a brief moment before flooding back worse than ever. Because Constance wasn't really her big sister. Yet another thing Penny would never have.

"I know Fortunato will help us once we tell him what happened to Chance," Constance was telling Howard. "And as soon as we get this all sorted out, we'll help you find Jack, too."

"Not me," Penny said. "I won't be of much use once I'm a marionette again."

She should have kept the bitter thought in her head. But she couldn't help it. She would do whatever she could to help Chance, because he did not deserve to spend eternity trapped in a puppet shell. But neither did Penny. She wanted to go see a show at the theater and eat steamed clams and crème brûlée and look at dinosaur bones and go to the carnival just to play games and ride rides.

It wasn't fair at all.

Constance stopped dead in her tracks, turned to Penny, and pulled her into a tight hug. "You will *always* be useful," she whispered fiercely. "Always. Okay? We're going to figure this out, I promise."

Penny had no idea how Constance could promise such a thing. But in that moment, she believed the girl with all her heart.

Howard smiled tentatively at her, and Penny smiled back. Then she noticed a sign taped to the lamppost just behind him. "That boy looks like you."

She pulled away from Constance, and they both stepped forward to get a better look at the sign. It read MISSING at the top in giant letters, with a picture of a younger version of Howard below that. At the bottom of the page, Penny read:

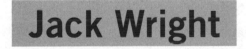

Jack Wright

Age: 10
Height: 4'4"
Weight: 65 lbs.

Last seen July 2 heading into
the park on the west side.

Contact police with any information.

Howard nodded. "That's Jack. He took it hard, my parents' car accident—we both did. But after a while, I started feeling better. He just got sadder and sadder. That's why everyone thinks he ran away, but I know he didn't. Something terrible must've . . ." He paused, swallowing hard. "I have to find him. I'll do anything."

His voice cracked a little, and suddenly he looked much older. Or maybe just more tired. Penny felt a pang of sadness as she glanced back at the photo of Jack. His eyes were wide and innocent. She wondered what had happened to him, but she was afraid to ask the question out loud. There were many possible answers, none of which were pleasant to ponder.

The three continued their trek to the museum, their mood more subdued now. Constance, still determinedly cheery despite everything that had happened, attempted to take their minds off it with chatter about what they might have to eat once they found Fortunato. It was late afternoon now, they'd devoured the last of the fruit in Constance's bag hours ago, and all three were increasingly distracted by thoughts of bacon and eggs, warm chocolate croissants, or peanut butter and banana sandwiches. By the time they rounded the final corner and saw the Museum of the Peculiar Arts up ahead, the gnawing in Penny's stomach and the pounding in her head made it difficult to feel triumphant or relieved or anything aside from slightly less irritated.

Constance fell silent as they crossed the street. It was as if the weight of the next few minutes had finally settled on them; if Fortunato was not here, they would have to confront the man with the sharp face alone. If they could even get into the carnival. Penny saw Constance cross her fingers with one hand as she reached for the door handle with the other. She hesitated for a second, then pulled.

The door opened, and Penny breathed a sigh of relief. She and Constance shared a smile as they entered, Howard right behind them.

Constance led the way, all of them keeping more quiet than seemed necessary, tiptoeing around the curio cabinets and hardly daring to breathe. Even though they had a good reason to be here, and Fortunato would certainly welcome them, Penny felt as though they were trespassing. But the door was unlocked, so surely *someone* was here. And sure enough, a voice suddenly sounded from the back.

"Watch that oak cabinet, now! It might be one of the cabinetmaker's, and you boys are about to scratch the magic right out of it."

A few chuckles followed this statement, along with the muffled thumps of boxes being dropped. Constance stopped walking abruptly and turned to face Penny. Her expression was screwed up in confusion, and Penny knew why. That voice didn't belong to Fortunato. She'd recognize it anywhere.

It belonged to the Storm.

SOMETHING FROM NOTHING

In Chance's favorite episode of *Storm at Dawn*, the sinister Madam M poisoned the Storm's tea with a draft that put him into a deathlike state. Though he appeared to be dead, eyes wide open and immobile, the Storm was actually fully conscious as he was mourned. Always prepared for the worst, the Storm knew his only chance for survival was to use the abilities he hadn't lost—sight and hearing—to their fullest extent.

Information is power, Chance told the Brave Knight. *The*

Storm always says that when you discover your enemy's secrets, you discover his weaknesses.

But even if we do learn something that can help us, then what? the knight replied. *We can't do anything about it. We can't move or talk to anyone except each other.*

And the puppeteer, Chance reminded him, remembering that moment in the museum when that sharp face had been so close to his, those long fingers grazing his strings. *But first things first. We need to learn everything we can about him if we're going to discover his weakness.*

And so they used what abilities they had. Because the Brave Knight's helmet severely limited what he could see, he focused on listening. He listened to the sounds of the children passing by the trailer, their voices growing hushed with excitement as they dared to approach the door, the shrieks and giggles as they ran away, unable to gather the courage to even knock. He listened to the quiet whir of the spinning wheel when the puppeteer would sit behind it, spinning and spinning despite the lack of string. He listened to the different rattling sounds the contents of each drawer made when the puppeteer would open and close them, and tried to discern what was inside.

Chance focused on looking. He looked at every tool the puppeteer used, each made with the same polished wood and near-translucent silver as the spindle, which had started all his troubles. He looked in all the cabinets the puppeteer opened, and memorized which ones he didn't. He looked at the puppeteer's expression every time he sat behind the spinning wheel, studied the way his face contorted in pain when his fingers became too stiff to continue.

The puppeteer's increasing frustration might have been frightening, but Chance was grateful for it. Because after every show, the puppeteer would shove the marionettes onto the shelf without taking the time to ensure their strings weren't touching: Princess Penny and the Brave Knight on the top shelf; the Sheepherder, the Wise Wizard, and the Evil Witch on the bottom shelf. Chance wondered if those marionettes were listening and looking and speaking to one another through their strings. Maybe they were even plotting.

Having the Brave Knight at his side helped Chance remember himself. He was not a marionette. He was a boy. And maybe this wasn't the adventure he'd wanted, but it was happening whether he liked it or not. He could save himself. He could still be a hero, like the Storm.

When the cabinet door was closed and there was nothing to hear or see, Chance and the knight discussed what all this information might mean. Their progress was hampered by the performances, of which there were seven a day; the first was at ten, and the others followed on the hour. The shows were only twenty minutes long, but they seemed to stretch on longer than the space between them, to the point where Chance all but forgot his real self and believed he was Princess Penny by the end. In the quiet dark of the cupboard afterward, bits and pieces of his former life would eventually trickle back as he talked with the Brave Knight.

They discussed the spinning wheel more than anything else.

Why does he just spin like he's expecting something from nothing? the knight wondered.

Maybe it's supposed to spin something from nothing, Chance replied. *Like magic.*

Suddenly, an image began floating across the surface of Chance's mind. He and the knight quieted their thoughts and waited. They had grown accustomed to this by now. A memory from Chance's real life would begin to take shape in the fog, and as soon as they sensed it, they both focused all their energy on not scaring it off.

The spindle the puppeteer had left in Chance's mail. Chance keenly recalled the sense of desperation he'd felt trying to reattach the string to Penny's head. He remembered the shock when the needle had suddenly sunk so easily into Penny's scalp. He remembered too the very real sensation of descending into foggy nothingness. And something else: a thought, an observation, but this part of the memory was bruised, discolored, harder to look at.

Chance and the knight focused as hard as they could. And then they both saw it, the strange thing Chance had noticed right before he'd passed out.

The string had been too long.

Much too long. Yards and yards of the stuff. Just like in a fairy tale, Chance had spun something from nothing—and he hadn't even used a spinning wheel. Just its spindle.

So, thought the knight. *Maybe the puppeteer is trying to spin string out of nothing?*

But string is practically worthless, Chance said. *It's not like spinning gold out of nothing.*

He had the nagging sensation that he hadn't seen all there was to see from that memory. As if he were on the brink of a revelation. If he were in his real, human body, Chance would no doubt be experiencing frustration. He was standing on the edge of an epiphany, and he couldn't take a step forward.

String's not worthless when you make marionettes for a living, the knight was saying. *Especially when those marionettes can talk through their strings. He needs the materials.*

Chance didn't respond. The *materials.* His thoughts were moving in overdrive now, making connections so fast he couldn't keep up with himself. The spinning wheel. The string. The cabinets filled with the shiny tools and all the materials the puppeteer needed to make his magical marionettes. Only, Chance had been so busy cataloging what he *saw,* he'd forgotten to consider what he *didn't* see. The realization hit like lightning.

Wood, he told the knight. *There's no wood in this trailer.*

THE STORM

Penny had never listened harder in her life.

Eyes closed, hardly daring to breathe, she stood with her back to a cabinet filled with vampire incisors labeled by country of origin. It was the Storm's voice, no question—but there was no static, no comforting radio-crackle.

He was *here*.

Other voices soon joined his, and then there were more sounds: shuffling, scraping. But Penny kept her attention on the Storm. Or rather, on the actor who played the Storm, A. P. Halls. He spoke differently as himself—less depth, less grandeur. And while the Storm always sounded wary, even of characters he trusted, A. P. Halls sounded friendly and kind.

"Penny. *Penny.*"

Startled, she turned to find Constance and Howard waving frantically at her and realized she had involuntarily stepped away from the cabinet. She wanted to talk to the Storm in person. After all that time she'd spent here on her shelf in this very museum listening to his stories, she felt as though she knew him intimately. It seemed wrong that he should not know her as well.

But of course, A. P. Halls would not see her—he would see Chance. And regardless, he probably wasn't interested in the personal lives of his fans. Penny forced herself to join Constance and Howard, who were now crouching behind a short glass cabinet.

"I can't believe this," Constance whispered, eyes alight with excitement. "What's the Storm doing here?"

Howard stood quietly and stretched onto his tiptoes, leaning to the side. Constance reached up and held on to his arm, as if to help him balance, although Penny didn't think it was necessary. She didn't let go when Howard crouched back down with them.

"There's a bunch of cables on the floor," he said softly. "Microphones and other stuff too."

"Did you see the Storm?" Penny asked, but he shook his head.

"I don't see anyone. And I don't even know what he looks like, do you?"

"No," Penny admitted. But she felt certain she would recognize him when she saw him.

The three of them stayed there for nearly a full minute, listening to the chatter and sounds of equipment being set up. Then Constance winced and got to her feet.

"My legs are cramping up," she told them. "Look, they're obviously not going anywhere, and we can't just hide here the rest of the day—we have to find Fortunato."

"Maybe he's with the Storm," Penny suggested. "They're using his museum, after all."

"It's not his museum anymore; he sold it." Constance blinked. "Oh! Maybe . . . do you think Mr. Halls bought it?"

The other two shrugged. "Can't we just ask him?" Penny wondered. "Why are we hiding at all?"

"Because . . ." Constance chewed her lip and glanced at Howard. "Well, the door was unlocked, so we didn't break in, exactly, but we're not supposed to be here. What if they call the police on us?"

The Storm would never do that, Penny wanted to say, but she didn't. Because she knew, logically, that the Storm was just a fictional character, and that A. P. Halls might very well call the police to report three runaway children sneaking around a closed museum.

Or he might help them find Fortunato.

"I know." Penny gestured for the others to lean closer.

"We should split up. One of us can go talk to the—to Mr. Halls and see if he knows where Fortunato is. The other two can keep hiding in case . . . well, in case things go wrong. Look," she added when Constance opened her mouth to protest. "If Mr. Halls can help us find Fortunato, then we're that much closer to finding Chance."

Constance pressed her lips together. It was clear she didn't like the idea of them separating, but Penny knew she had made a solid point. "Fine," Constance said at last. "So which of us talks to Mr. Halls?"

Penny thought that much was obvious. "Me, of course."

This time it was Howard who protested.

"No," he said, then looked at Constance. "It should be you."

Constance tilted her head. "Why?"

"Because you're . . . you look more . . ." Cheeks darkening, Howard waved his hand vaguely at her. "Innocent."

The corner of Constance's mouth twitched. "Because I'm a girl?"

"Well, yes." Howard glanced at Penny and shrugged. "Adults are just that way, you know? People see us boys at the park without anyone watching us, they usually assume we're up to no good. But with the girls? They get all concerned, ask if they're lost. Especially, um . . . well, especially white girls. That's just how it is."

That was impossibly stupid, in Penny's opinion. But

then she remembered how the police chief had had patience with Constance but not with Howard, even though they had both been guilty of the same wrongdoing and they had both called him "sir" so politely. She remembered how the Bonvillains had acted as though the idea of Chance having dolls was laughable, whereas it was normal for his sister. She remembered how the Thank-You Man had leered at Constance and taken obvious pleasure in her fear, all while ignoring the brother at her side.

Howard was right, Penny realized. But she didn't understand why. They all had brains and hearts; those were the most important bits. Why should it matter if some of their other parts were different?

Constance was nodding in agreement. "You're right," she said, and now her hand was back on Howard's arm. He did not seem to mind. "But if we're separated . . . Penny . . . I can't just—"

"I'll take care of her," Howard told her. "I promise. We'll do everything we can to find your brother."

He gave her a nervous but reassuring smile, which Constance returned. Penny supposed she should have felt irritated that they had made this decision without her, even though the idea had been hers. But that feeling was back more powerfully than ever—the one she could only guess was specific to children who had older siblings. That warm feeling of being safe and protected and cared for. She felt that same tugging in her chest as she had earlier, as if something were trying to get her attention but she couldn't quite see it.

Constance smoothed out her skirt, straightened her back, and marched out from behind the cabinet. Howard and Penny crouched down, tensed and ready to run.

"Excuse me," they heard Constance say, her voice bright and polite. "I was looking for Mr. Fortunato?"

A little thrill sang through Penny's chest when the Storm responded. "I'm afraid he doesn't work here anymore," he said. "Did you know him?"

"Oh yes, he's a dear friend of my dad's," Constance replied. "I just love this museum. I can't believe it's gone!"

"Not for long!" a new voice chimed in, this one belonging to a woman. "My brother and I bought the place and most of Fortunato's stock along with it. We've got quite a collection of our own, too. And my brother thought getting the Storm himself to broadcast live from the museum would be great publicity for our grand reopening!"

Penny frowned. Fortunato had sold his oddities, too? She had assumed everything was going into storage. His collection was all he had; why would he sell it?

"How exciting!" Constance was saying. "You don't happen to know where Fortunato's gone, do you? It's very important that I find him."

"He moved out early this morning," said the woman. "Heading for the carnival."

Penny and Howard exchanged a wide-eyed look.

"The carnival?" Constance asked innocently. "You mean, just for the day?"

A. P. Halls responded, only now he sounded every bit like the Storm: sad and wary.

"Oh no. He's taking over for the puppeteer."

THE FIRST STEP

The late-afternoon sun still burned strong as the curtain rose for the Princess Penny show once again. The star of the show relished every moment onstage, every twirl and leap, every sight that wasn't cupboard doors. He lost himself in the story once again, all memories of his parents and his sister and the real Penny drifting farther down into the murky waters of his mind. Each time, those memories took longer to resurface after the performance. He wondered vaguely how long it would be before they drowned completely, and whether that would really be so terrible.

It might have happened that very evening had he not suddenly seen Fortunato.

The former owner of the Museum of the Peculiar Arts stood under the shade of a nearby oak tree, watching. It wasn't until near the end of the show, when Princess Penny and the Brave Knight were rushing from the caves, that a familiar silvery head appeared in the distance. Suddenly, the memory of an emotion returned: anger, red and raw and real.

The princess clung to the memory of that feeling throughout the rest of the show as the Evil Witch was destroyed and good prevailed. He clung to it during the song of gratitude and during the final dance through the field of flowers. The children watching had no idea that the beautiful princess spinning and singing so joyfully on the outside was very close to seething with rage on the inside.

As a rule, the puppeteer did not socialize with his adoring audiences after performances. But he would leave the five marionettes hanging from the rafters in artful poses, their toes just skimming the stage, and allow the children to come and admire them up close for a few minutes. Eyes sparkling with wonder and curiosity, they would lean as far as they dared over the stage, taking in the exquisite details of each marvelous puppet, reaching out but never daring to touch. Most children had their fill after a minute or two of staring, and then the distant shouts of laughter and tinkling music would beckon them to return to the carnival's other delights. But one or two usually lingered, unable to look away from the puppets. Often these children seemed lonely or lost. Sometimes even desperate. The puppeteer, lurking in the shadows of the curtain, would memorize their faces and identify those who were saddest.

Sadness was a vital step in creating the world's most marvelous lifelike, life-size marionettes.

It was, in fact, the first step.

184

HER PUPPET SHELL

"The puppeteer?"

Penny stepped out from behind the cabinet, ignoring Howard's frantic whispers to stay hidden. Her eyes were locked on the Storm. He wasn't nearly as tall as she'd imagined: he was pale and slight, with dark eyes that seemed kind but were creased with worry lines. He was younger than she'd expected too—younger than the Bonvillain parents. He glanced at Penny, then did a double take.

Kinship, that unexpected jolt of recognition when seeing a bit of yourself reflected in the eyes of a stranger.

For a moment, Penny's logic and reason vanished. The Storm *did* know her. Not Chance. *Her*. Somehow, impossibly, he knew her just as well as she knew him.

Then the Storm said, "And who's this?" and Penny's heart sank. She glanced at Constance, who cleared her throat.

"This is my brother, Joey. And I'm Jessica. *Joey*," Constance said firmly, giving Penny a pointed look, "you don't have to be shy. Come meet Mr. Halls."

Penny stepped forward, still unable to look away from the Storm. She was vaguely aware of a few other adults watching, standing among a mess of cords and cables and unfamiliar equipment. The Storm shook her hand, and she swallowed nervously.

He smiled. "Nice to meet you, Joey."

The way he said "Joey" was strange, as if he knew that wasn't her real name. Constance fidgeted nervously, and Penny wondered if she'd screwed everything up. Her brain seemed to have split into two parts: the logical side, which was berating her decision to step forward and was frantically trying to assess what to do if Mr. Halls realized they were runaways; and a newfound dreamy side, which insisted that this man was, in fact, the Storm and that he could help them save Chance. He was always the hero of the story, after all.

"So," the Storm said. "You two have heard of the puppeteer?"

"Just old stories, sir," Constance replied, while Penny merely shook her head. But in truth, the word alone conjured vague images that drifted through her mind like smoke; graceful, long-fingered hands, icy blue eyes, and hollow smiles. Music, too—a tinkling melody she couldn't quite hum.

"Fortunato knows him," the Storm said. He seemed to be choosing his words carefully. "I assume you know the old tale of the cabinetmaker's apprentice?"

He glanced at Penny, who nodded mutely. "Yes, sir," Constance squeaked.

"The puppeteer modeled his marionettes after that story," the Storm continued. "Brought him fame for a brief time. Then he disappeared—drafted into the war, or at least that's what everyone believes. He came back, but he was changed. And not for the better. Like seeing the worst of humanity made him less human."

Penny's breathing grew shallow. The man with the sharp face, the puppeteer; she knew deep in her gut they were one and the same. The same man who had cut off her string and kidnapped Chance.

He had created her.

"He gave his last marionette to Fortunato ages ago, before he went overseas. When he returned, he began to build more. And now he's about to turn all of them—his whole show—over to Fortunato."

The Storm's words washed over Penny in waves, drowning

her. The logical part of her brain was shrinking by the second, but she still heard it: *Why does this matter? Why are you panicking? Just focus on finding Chance!*

Even Constance's voice trembled a bit when she spoke. "But why?"

"That's a good question," the Storm said. "I wish I knew the answer. But I do know this—he's dangerous. My advice to you two is to stay far, far away from him."

"We weren't . . . I . . . not going to . . . ," Constance sputtered. But the Storm wasn't looking at her. Constance fell silent as he leaned down, looked Penny right in the eyes, and whispered:

"How long have you been swapped?"

The world stopped moving. Penny's shock was so great that she didn't feel it at first: no sharp intake of breath, no extra-hard *thump* of the heart. It was as though time were suspended.

The moment was broken when the Storm, with an encouraging smile, placed his hand on her shoulder and said, "It's okay." Then relief flooded through Penny, shaking her limbs and rattling her rib cage and causing her eyes to leak. She sank to the floor, and Constance was at her side in an instant with a comforting hand on her back. The Storm sat cross-legged in front of Penny. The other adults continued setting up behind them, apparently unaware that the entire universe had just collapsed into particles and rearranged itself into something entirely different.

"How did you know?" Penny whispered.

The Storm took a few seconds to answer. "I met the puppeteer once," he said at last. "At the carnival when I was a little boy. I didn't have any family—none who wanted me, anyway—and after the show, I went up to the stage to look at the marionettes more closely. One in particular caught my attention. She had blue hair." He smiled wistfully. "When I touched her strings and heard her voice, I was just . . . enchanted."

Penny shifted uncomfortably. She carefully avoided looking at Constance's expression.

Perhaps the Storm had read her mind, because he added: "I know, I know. *The Cabinetmaker's Apprentice* has it all wrong. She was no soul thief."

He paused, and Penny squeezed her hands in her lap, silently willing him to continue.

"It's hard for me to explain, even now," he went on softly. "I held her strings, and suddenly we were on a seesaw, tilting back and forth between child and puppet." The Storm glanced at Penny. "Like I could lend a bit of my realness to her and borrow her puppetness in exchange. Does that make sense?"

Penny nodded, picturing that moment when she and Chance had practiced in front of the mirror. She had felt almost alive, twirling of her own accord, while Chance's eyes had gone glassy, his arms stiff.

"Yes," she whispered.

Constance, however, was shaking her head. "But that sounds like she *did* steal your soul, or she was trying to."

"It wasn't about taking," the Storm replied. "It was about giving. And if anyone was a thief," he added with a sigh, "it was me. The puppeteer frightened me, but I couldn't bear to leave her behind . . . so I stole her. I stole her and ran away, and later I told everyone the puppeteer had given her to me. I lied."

Constance spoke through her fingers, which were pressed to her lips. "Did he come after you?"

"I assume he did. But I found a place to hide for nearly a year. When I left, the carnival was in the city again, but the puppeteer was no longer a part of it. This summer is the first anyone's seen of him since then."

Penny took a deep breath. She should not ask the next question. She should not, because she suspected she knew the answer. But she had to hear it.

"Where is your marionette now?"

The Storm glanced away. But not before Penny saw a flash of guilt in his eyes. And that was all the answer she needed. It didn't matter if his marionette was packed away in a box or sitting on a dusty shelf. What mattered was that she was alone. Trapped in her puppet shell forever. A boy who'd once loved her so much that he'd stolen her from the puppeteer had grown up into a man who had no time for dolls.

Terror seized Penny as she realized this would no doubt be her fate too. She wondered if that marionette ever regretted not keeping the body of A. P. Halls. She could have lived a real life, and no one would ever have known what she'd done.

In that moment, Penny decided she would not make the same mistake.

She struggled to stand, her decision weighing her down. "I have to use the bathroom," she announced loudly, and both Mr. Halls and Constance looked surprised. "Will you excuse me, please?"

Mr. Halls said, "Of course." Constance stared questioningly at Penny. But Penny ignored her. She felt sure that if Constance looked her in the eyes for even a second, she would see what was in Penny's heart right now.

She would know that maybe Penny was a demon after all.

Penny walked in the direction of the little washroom next to Fortunato's office. Then she slipped behind a cabinet and scurried through the rows, staying at a crouch and making her way to the front door. She was almost there when a hand grabbed her shoulder, and she spun around with a gasp.

Howard's eyes were wide. "Where are you going?" he whispered. The *thump-thump-thump* of her heartbeat filled Penny's ears. Shame coursed through her, but it wasn't enough to make her change her mind.

"I really hope you find your brother," she said, her voice cracking. Then she pulled out of his grasp and took off sprinting down the street toward the park.

HOPE

The puppeteer had been in the spinning-wheel cabinet for hours. Fortunato was busying himself around the trailer, opening and closing drawers, examining tools, avoiding the accusatory gazes of the marionettes, which lined the shelf above him, strings deliberately separated. He'd closed the cabinet doors for a while, then opened them again, as if the guilt of shutting the marionettes up in the dark was too much to bear. The former museum owner seemed nervous and distracted, and after nearly an hour of poking around, he turned on the small portable radio he'd set on the table earlier.

A woman's voice filled the trailer, bright and peppy as she babbled about her favorite brand of soap. Chance only half heard the advertisement. The atmosphere was crackling with tension, as if something big were about to happen. It was all Chance could do to remember who Fortunato was, much less imagine what he might be planning. The process of thinking had become a trek through a swamp that grew deeper and murkier with every step. Sinking into it was inevitable, especially without the Brave Knight to help pull him through, and every few minutes Chance would decide there was no point in fighting. Then his gaze would refocus on Fortunato, and an echo of his earlier anger would give him the strength to take another step, and another.

The advertisement ended, and a few familiar, eerie chords sounded from the radio.

"A storm is brewing. Are YOU prepared for the worst?"

Chance stopped thinking. He stood stock-still in his mind swamp, not sinking, not moving at all. This moment was achingly familiar . . . here with Fortunato as he worked, listening to *Storm at Dawn*. Only now he was on this shelf, watching. Just like Penny used to do.

"Tonight, on Storm at Dawn, *we're broadcasting live from the recently closed Museum of the Peculiar Arts."*

Fortunato froze, staring at the radio.

"It's a peculiar place indeed, filled with strange objects and stranger secrets. In fact, dear listeners, it's the inspiration behind tonight's tale, titled . . . 'The Thief of Souls.'"

The door to the spinning-wheel cabinet burst open and slammed against the wall, sending a tremor through the trailer. The puppeteer stood framed in the doorway, breathing heavily, his perfectly carved face contorted in anger.

"The villain I faced in this adventure was unlike any I'd encountered before. He was a gifted thief, one who could look you in the eyes as he stole your most valuable possession. How? Because you never realized he was taking it by force. In fact, he would convince you that you'd given it to him of your own free will . . . and then you would forget it was ever yours to begin with."

In three great strides, the puppeteer crossed the trailer and flipped the radio off. His shoulders rose and fell, and he massaged the spot on his neck where once there'd been a wart. There was no indentation now, no indication whatsoever that he'd violently hacked it off that morning.

The seconds stretched on too long, silent and tense. Quietly the puppeteer closed the door to the spinning-wheel cabinet. He removed a small black box from his cloak pocket, which he set on the table. When he spoke at last, his voice was like the wind whistling through the tree branches outside.

"She'll be here soon. I'll make sure of it." He headed to the door, pulled it open, and looked back at Fortunato. "Have everything ready before I return."

He didn't wait for Fortunato's response before sweeping out the door. It clicked shut loudly. A moment later, Fortunato drew a long, shaky breath. He opened the small black box and peered inside. Chance could not see its contents, but Fortunato visibly shuddered. He pushed the box out of Chance's sight, then turned the radio back on.

"This was a dangerous enemy, to be certain. Because how can you fight for what is yours if you have no memory of it at all? One word, dear listeners: hope. When you—"

There was a distant cry and a shuffling sound. Fortunato stared at the radio, his expression as bewildered as Chance felt. Because this did not sound like part of the show. And then a girl's voice came through the speakers. Teary but bright and full of optimism.

Constance.

"Chance, if you're listening to this, I'm coming for you. I promise I'll—"

What happened next, Chance would later play over and over again in his mind.

Emotions surged through him at the sound of his sister's voice. Relief, and hope, and love—not a memory, but *real*. And though it was impossible, though he was nothing more than a soul trapped in wood, Chance instinctively tried to fling himself at the radio.

Fortunato's hip bumped the table, shaking the shelf. Chance toppled from his spot and sprawled on top of the radio, which was now emitting nothing but static silence. A few seconds passed. Then Fortunato picked him up with trembling hands and placed him back on the shelf. He straightened each of the other marionettes in turn, taking

195

care not to touch any of their strings. He smoothed down his apron. Then he went back to digging around in cupboards and cabinets with greater fervor, as if he were looking for something important.

He turned the radio off.

Chance's thoughts were racing faster than they had in days. His sister knew he was in trouble. She was coming for him. And that knowledge had given Chance the strength to do the impossible. Because Fortunato might have bumped the shelf, but the other marionettes had not fallen. And Chance knew why.

He had *moved*.

And if he could do it once, he could do it again.

29

AN AMAZING SENSE TO POSSESS

The sun had finally set, but the streets were by no means deserted. Penny darted from one block to the next, mimicking Constance's zigzagging pattern from earlier that day. With every hour that passed, her guilt over running away grew stronger. But she ignored the twist in her gut. The logical part of her brain was in charge again. And it didn't matter that Constance seemed to care for Penny. It didn't matter that Chance had promised that Penny would never be packed away into storage. These were the facts:

Once Chance and Penny swapped back, he and Constance

would age. Penny would not. She would be a marionette forever. And adults, like the Storm, did not keep the promises they made to puppets when they were children, no matter how much they claimed to love them.

Penny would never be in charge of her own future. Not unless she stole Chance's body.

She turned onto a quiet street and broke into a run, slowing only when a couple strolled out of a restaurant hand in hand. A block down to her right, Penny could see the edge of the park. Nodding to herself, she darted around the couple and turned left. She didn't know the city like Constance did, but she was certain she was heading north. Back to the neighborhood where she and Constance had woken up that morning.

Back to Club Heavenly Blues.

It was ridiculously foolish to go back there. A child should not roam the city streets alone when night was falling, and the club was dozens of blocks away. A vision of Mrs. Goldstein's concerned face flashed through Penny's mind, and she felt another pang of guilt. She remembered the leering Thank-You Man, and the police chief who questioned them at the station, and the kind nun who clearly had not wanted to let them leave the church. Constance had gotten them out of all those situations with her quick thinking. She had not seemed afraid, not like Penny was right now.

Puppets were completely dependent on their puppeteer. But right now Penny was more independent than she had ever been. Every decision, every move, was her choice.

It was terrifying.

It was *wonderful.*

She ran in short sprints, slowing to examine a rosebush or pick up a shiny coin. She leaped up onto a park bench and peered over the fence surrounding the park, then jumped off the bench, enjoying the shock that shot up through her knees when her feet smacked onto the pavement. She used the coin she'd found to buy a small bag of roasted nuts, which were sugary and salty and made her cry because taste was an amazing sense to possess.

She hopped on one foot, then the other. She spun in circles until she was dizzy. She ran block after block until her sides ached and her lungs felt ready to burst, and it was glorious—almost glorious enough to distract her from the truth of what she was doing.

But she could not outrun the guilt.

It found her when she reached the north end of the park and turned onto 110th Street. Penny flew past a lamppost, then skidded to a halt so fast she nearly fell over. Panting, she stumbled back to the post and stared at the MISSING poster.

This one wasn't for Howard's brother, Jack. It was for a boy and girl. Linda and Lyle Goldstein, according to the poster: twins, nine years old, white skin, blond hair, blue eyes. They were last seen near the park earlier in the spring.

Goldstein? The kind older couple had said nothing about children, or grandchildren. And it was a common enough last name. But then Penny remembered how Mrs.

Goldstein had been so concerned about her and Constance's safety, how determined she'd been that they not wander off alone, how she'd gone right to a police officer. . . .

Penny's breath was still coming in deep, shaky gasps. Howard's brother, Jack, had gone missing near the park too. And hadn't the police chief mentioned that Jack wasn't the only child who'd disappeared? A sense of foreboding settled in her stomach like a stone at the bottom of a well. It was as if deep down she knew exactly what had happened to these children, but the truth was too dark and too terrible, and her mind refused to let her see it.

Linda and Lyle were lost. So was Jack. There was little Penny could do about that.

But she could do something about Chance.

Penny squeezed her eyes closed, but not before a tear escaped, leaving a cold trail down her cheek. Constance would say there was always a bright side, and in Penny's case, it was this:

Once she was a marionette again, she wouldn't have to feel sadness anymore. She wouldn't feel anything.

Nodding to herself, Penny opened her eyes. She squared her shoulders. And she marched into the park, heading south toward the closed-up carnival, oblivious to the dark figure that shadowed her.

OBVIOUSLY A TRAP

"That was crazy. That was really crazy, what you just did."

Constance grinned, because the way Howard said it sounded more like admiration than criticism. The two of them were just inside the park, leaning against a tree and trying to catch their breath.

She supposed Howard was right. Her mother certainly wouldn't have approved of what her daughter had just done. But right before his show began, Mr. Halls had pulled Constance aside and given her a piece of advice.

"Stay away from the puppeteer. I know you think you can save your brother, but trust me—it's too late."

Constance did not get angry very often, but those words had sparked a little red knot of fury she usually managed to contain, balled up tight in her chest. Only on rare occasions was it difficult for her to control. Like when strange men leered at her just to see her squirm, then forced her to thank them for "help" she'd never requested. Or when teachers wrote *sweet disposition* on her progress reports with no mention of her intelligence. Or when her parents didn't recognize an impostor in place of their own son.

Those moments, those people, they made Constance feel like a shell with nothing inside. She might as well have been a marionette.

And then A. P. Halls, the Storm himself, her brother's hero, had told her to leave Chance to his doom. To be a good girl and go home.

She'd smiled politely and nodded and watched as Mr. Halls had sat behind the microphone and started talking about a villain he'd based on the puppeteer, a man who'd stolen her brother's *soul,* and that little knot of fury had swelled and boiled and raged and, inevitably, exploded.

Constance had snatched the microphone from Mr. Halls and shouted a message. Not just for her brother, but for the Storm, and for Fortunato, and for the puppeteer, even though she had no way of knowing if they could hear. She shouted it for A. P. Halls, to show him how badly he'd misjudged her. She shouted it for herself, because maybe sometimes a girl just needed to be loud. Be *heard*.

And then she ran.

"Some people do bad things," Constance told Howard now. "And some people think they're good, but they turn their heads and allow those bad things to happen. So they're just as bad, aren't they?"

Howard nodded fervently. "Yes. They are."

Tucking a loose strand of hair behind her ear, Constance did a quick survey of the park. The city streets were nowhere near deserted, but the park was quiet and still. A few more steps in and the trees would block the sight of the surrounding skyscrapers.

"We should get going," Constance said. "Penny might be there already."

Now Howard looked troubled. He didn't speak for nearly a full minute as they headed down the path that would take them to the carnival. Then he cleared his throat. "Constance, I . . . I really don't think she's coming. I think she ran away."

Constance smiled. "I know. But she'll change her mind."

"How do you know that?"

"Because it's the right thing to do."

Howard gave her a sideways glance. "Not everyone does the right thing. Look at the Storm."

"True. But Penny will."

Constance could tell Howard didn't believe her. But it

didn't matter. Penny was not like A. P. Halls. She might be frightened; she might even be angry—and she had every reason to be; but she was not the type who sacrificed others to save herself. Constance was absolutely sure of it.

When they reached the wall that served as a border for the carnival, Constance led the way around until they found the empty ticket-taker booth. Howard gave her a boost, and she scrambled over the turnstile, then held out her hand to help him. Afterward neither of them let go.

They marched through the silent carnival hand in hand, past all the closed-up booths and vendors, stopping occasionally to read the signs pointing to various attractions. They passed the Ferris wheel and the fun house, the Tilt-A-Whirl and the spinning teacups. Constance's favorite ride was the swings that rose high into the air and swung you in circles so fast you were almost parallel to the ground. Chance would insist that there was a possibility the chains could break, but he always rode them with her anyway.

At last Howard squeezed her hand and pointed. "Look."

The puppeteer's trailer sat beneath an elm tree, a few low-hanging branches nearly obscuring the sign. It was dark and still and silent, but the curtain was pulled up, revealing the cave scenery. And there was something hanging there, right in the middle of the stage.

The Princess Penny marionette looked exactly as Constance remembered, only now she was in a princess gown and tiara. Her eyes glinted in the moonlight, and Constance's heart leaped.

"Chance."

She stepped forward, but Howard pulled her back. "How can you be sure that's him? If the puppeteer swapped him once, he might have done it again."

Constance shook her head, her gaze still on the marionette. "I know my brother when I see him."

Howard glanced at the stage. "Even if it is him, this is obviously a trap. That . . . that puppet, it's bait. We have to come up with a plan."

"A plan?" Constance repeated. "This *was* the plan. We come to the trailer, get my brother, and make Fortunato swap him back with Penny."

"Penny ran away!" Howard exclaimed. "Look, Constance, I hope you're right and she does come back, but she's not here now, and—"

"You said you would do anything to get your brother back," Constance cut in quietly. "Did you mean it?"

Howard's eyes flashed. "Yes."

"Then you understand," Constance said. "My brother is on that stage. I know it's deliberate. And I don't care. I *want* the puppeteer to find me. I want to find *him*. I'm not going to hide or sneak around. I'm going to get my brother." She pulled her hand from his, patted him gently on the arm to show she wasn't mad, then turned and walked to the stage.

The soft crunch of grass under her feet seemed amplified. The park was unnaturally quiet: no crickets chirping,
no wind whistling through the leaves. It was as if a bubble
surrounded the trailer and muted the outside world. Constance placed her hands on the stage and heaved herself
up. When she faced the marionette at last, tears filled her
eyes. This was no princess puppet. This was her brother,
and she would recognize him anywhere.

"Hi, Chance," she whispered.

She heard a distant shout just before the curtain fell behind her, leaving them in absolute darkness.

THE CABINETMAKER'S
LEGENDARY CHAMBERS

One moment Chance was staring into his sister's face—and she'd recognized him, she'd *seen* him—and the next moment, total blackness. A void, empty of all light and sound.

It lasted for what seemed like eternity, or maybe it was only a few seconds. When the light returned, it blazed so bright that Chance briefly thought the trailer had exploded. Then it dimmed, and he gazed out of his marionette eyes in awe.

He was no longer on the stage. In fact, he couldn't be in the puppeteer's trailer at all. A huge cast-iron stove sat cold and empty across from where Chance sat. There was no source of light that he could see—no lamp, no lantern, not even a candle—yet the room was lit. It was the cabinets, Chance realized. The cabinets made of patchwork wood, oak and cherry and cedar and pine, all emitting a soft glow. There were too many to count.

The spinning wheel sat near one of the doors. Chance gazed at it, wondering why it had been moved from its cabinet in the puppeteer's trailer. The one cabinet that had always seemed much, much larger on the inside, as if the darkness expanded far beyond what the logics of physics and space would allow.

This *was* the spinning-wheel cabinet, Chance realized. No, it was more than that.

This was the cabinetmaker's legendary chambers.

Questions surged through Chance's mind, and he felt as though he could thread them together in a way that would provide answers if he tried hard enough. The puppeteer had told Fortunato the truth; the chambers had not been destroyed in the great fire. But Fortunato was the cabinetmaker's adopted son—surely he would have inherited all of this. But instead, the puppeteer had the chambers. Why?

Because he'd stolen them. Chance's thoughts were racing now, snapping puzzle pieces into place with a speed possessed only by marionettes, who had nothing but time to think. The puppeteer had stolen the cabinetmaker's chambers, just as the story said the cabinetmaker's apprentice had stolen his magical tools . . . tools he'd used to make puppets that took the souls of children.

The puppeteer was the cabinetmaker's apprentice.

It was so obvious, and yet impossible. Because even if that story was true, the real cabinetmaker had died decades ago at a ripe old age. Fortunato had been a little boy, and he was an old man now. If the cabinetmaker's apprentice were still alive, he'd be ancient, a wrinkled, warty, white-haired, shriveled husk of a man.

The puppeteer did not have a single wrinkle or wart.

Because he sliced them off. But how was he able to do that without drawing so much as a drop of blood? And how, *how* had he lived this long?

A distant voice interrupted Chance from these disturbing questions. It was too muffled for him to make out the words, but the voice was bright and strong and achingly familiar.

Constance.

Not being able to see her was beyond frustrating. The complacency Chance had begun to feel for his situation was gone, and now he felt exactly as he had in his first moments inside this marionette: terrified, paralyzed, desperately wanting to claw his way out of this prison.

Maybe he could.

Chance focused on the sound of his sister's voice. He summoned all his energy, focused his whole mind on the idea of moving. Just an inch. A centimeter, even. It felt like trying to move fog, but he pushed, and pushed, and *pushed*.

And then, covering the imperceptible distance of a hair, but a distance nonetheless . . . the marionette tilted forward.

The shock of it broke Chance's focus. He could see a bit more of the table below him now. On it lay the small black box the puppeteer had set out earlier. Inside was a coil of string. It was grayish and lacked the luster of the marionettes' strings.

This string isn't string at all.

Chance remembered the way Fortunato had shuddered when he peered inside the box. He remembered the way the spindle had helped him spin string out of seemingly nothing. He remembered the way the puppeteer would sit behind the spinning wheel, spinning and spinning as if expecting string to appear.

A cabinet door slammed open and the walls shook. The marionette leaned forward an inch, and then another, and then it was in a free fall. Chance watched the coil of string barrel at him, and suddenly, with great clarity, the revelation he'd felt on the verge of a hundred times finally hit him, both literally and figuratively.

The marionettes' strings are their souls.

He fell face-first onto the puppeteer's dull gray strings— his *soul*—and in one horrifying instant, the real story of the cabinetmaker's apprentice unfolded in Chance's mind. And he knew, without a doubt, that there was no way to escape the fate this villain had in store for him.

But Chance could still be a hero.

THE REAL STORY

There was once a cabinetmaker with an apprentice, and this apprentice was not a soul-thieving demon.

Not at first.

This boy worked hard to learn the skills that went into creating such wonderful cabinets. He knew the secret was in the cabinetmaker's tools; each one, from the smallest screwdriver to the most ornate scroll saw, seemed weighted with magic, just like the objects in the fairy tales he'd loved when he was very small. He spent countless happy hours with the cabinetmaker, learning the art of woodwork.

But while he was an obedient assistant and eager student, he could not seem to master the craft. One day the cabinetmaker told him the true secret of his trade.

"They are indeed good tools," he said, placing a hand on his apprentice's shoulder. "But the real magic comes from the hands that wield them. Trees are living things, and their wood contains their life energy. It's not the tools that coax that energy out. The tree must give it willingly."

The apprentice frowned. "But how can I make them do that?"

"You can't *make* them," the cabinetmaker replied with a gentle smile. "You must *ask*. That is the next step in your training."

But the apprentice was older now and far less patient. His cabinets were sturdy enough, and some were even beautiful, but none possessed the magical properties of the cabinetmaker's.

We use wood from the same trees, the apprentice thought sourly. *The magic isn't in the wood after all—it's in the tools. That's why he wants to keep them for himself.*

And so one day, the apprentice left the cabinetmaker's workshop with a sack filled with stolen tools and set out to create his own wonders.

He refurnished an abandoned trailer to be his workshop, then began to create things he was certain would bring him fame and fortune, magical objects straight from fairy tales: staffs and axes, bows and arrows, wands and mirrors.

Each, he assured his customers, contained astounding magical properties. But in truth, he could not coax the life energy from the trees. His creations were nothing but trinkets made of wood and glass and steel and not a single ounce of magic.

Save for one.

The apprentice set about building a spinning wheel out of the cabinetmaker's tools, carving chisels into spokes and levels into pedals. He topped it off with a sliver of the cabinetmaker's favorite saw, now a spindle that shone in a most entrancing way. He gave the wheel a spin and found himself spellbound. Excitement and pride bloomed in his chest, for at last he had built something that rivaled even the cabinetmaker's work!

But only, he realized, because he had used the tools he'd stolen from the cabinetmaker.

An odd mix of emotions churned in his chest. The tools didn't matter. Wasn't that what the old man had always said? But this spinning wheel was magical—the puppeteer could feel it. Desperate to prove his former master a liar, he took his masterpiece to the cabinetmaker's chambers and left it there for him to find.

Unfortunately, the orphans found it first.

Late that night, there came a pounding on the apprentice's trailer door. He opened it to find the cabinetmaker, red-faced and sobbing with grief and anger.

"How could you do that to her?" the old man wailed, thrusting the spinning wheel at the apprentice. "She was already so sad . . . so *sad.*" And before the apprentice could respond, his former master drew his last breath and collapsed.

The apprentice did not know what to make of this. Until he paid a visit to the cabinetmaker's chambers early the next morning and found the orphans curled up on the floor, asleep.

No. The boy was asleep. The girl, though . . .

Creeping closer as softly as possible, the apprentice stared at the girl in wonder. For she was no longer a girl at all. Gently, gently, the apprentice extracted the sleeping boy's grip from his sister's arms. He carried the boy to a nearby church, deposited him neatly on its doorstep, and then returned to the cabinetmaker's chambers.

His chambers now.

But the apprentice was no longer interested in building cabinets or fairy-tale objects. This hollow shell of a girl, this perfect puppet with her shiny strings, this was his key to fame and fortune.

The apprentice experimented with his spinning wheel for years and years. But try as he might, he could not figure out exactly how the orphaned girl had become a marionette. Then, when decades had passed and his skin was far more wrinkled than he would have liked, another girl arrived.

This girl had recently experienced a great and terrible loss, and she was desperate for a place to hide from her miserable life. The apprentice noticed her lurking behind a tree when he left the chambers one morning, then slipping inside when she thought he was out of sight. She gazed around in awe at the cabinets filled with curiosities. But it was the spinning wheel that called to her.

The girl knew all about spinning wheels from fairy tales. Stories filled with helpless damsels in distress. She was in great distress and had little hope that help would ever arrive. But she sat down behind the wheel and began to spin.

She pedaled and pedaled, and though nothing happened, her sadness began to fade. And after some time, she noticed that string had appeared on the wheel. She spun faster and faster and watched as more string appeared, hypnotized by the sight of her soul unraveling.

The apprentice, peering through a crack in the door, was hypnotized too.

Soon a lifelike, life-size marionette slumped over the spinning wheel. Its chin had been nicked on the spindle, and a few severed fingers lay on the floor—now brittle and hard like twigs that had gotten caught in the spokes.

The apprentice examined this new curiosity, marveling at the details. This puppet was as magical as the first. And now he understood the secret of the spinning wheel.

She was so sad.

The apprentice had lived a long life, and it was nearing its natural end. This wasn't fair. At last he knew how to create the most incredible lifelike, life-size marionettes the world would ever see, just as death was on its way to greet him.

The unfairness of it all was too much to bear. The apprentice seethed. He screamed. He wept.

Then he grabbed a pair of scissors, sat behind the wheel, and began to spin.

His soul bled out in shiny wisps. He worked slowly, methodically, wrapping it around and around the spindle. He welcomed the numbness and descended into the fog, stopping frequently to regain his focus. He would not lose himself completely, as those stupid girls had done.

When he had spun out as much as he could bear, he picked up the scissors and snipped the strings loose.

They shimmered as they drifted to the floor, then turned a dull, muted gray. The apprentice locked them in a small black box. He studied his reflection in the mirror, pressed a knife tentatively to his wrinkled cheek, experimented with a small slice.

He felt nothing.

Once he'd carved his age away, he turned his attention to the broken-fingered marionette. *Truly remarkable,* he thought, setting it next to the other on a shelf. His key to fame and fortune, indeed. No puppet show would compare to his, not with life-size, lifelike marionettes as incredible as these, even if one was a bit damaged.

Of course, to put on a proper show, he would need more than two puppets. But that wouldn't be a problem, he knew. For there would always be children in the world who were sad.

This was the moment he ceased to be an apprentice. He was the puppeteer, and he had a collection to build.

UNRAVELING

Penny peered through the bushes at the puppeteer's trailer. A shadowy figure darted around it, first checking the empty stage, then pushing on all the knobless doors. Not the puppeteer. A tall, familiar boy.

"Howard?"

The boy whirled around, hands up in the air as if she'd caught him stealing. He lowered them slowly as she approached, his expression a mix of relief and surprise.

"You ran away."

He didn't say it in a particularly accusatory way, but Penny still flinched. "I changed my mind."

Howard nodded slowly. "Constance was right. She said you'd come back."

You aren't a demon. Penny squeezed her eyes closed briefly. She did not have much longer in this borrowed body, and she couldn't return it to Chance with a wet face. "Where *is* Constance?"

She listened as Howard explained how they had seen the marionette hanging over the stage, how Constance had climbed up to get it, how the curtain had fallen. Howard had hurried forward to pull it up, but they were gone. Like a magician's vanishing act.

"They're in the trailer," Penny said dully. The thrill of knowing she was so close to rescuing Chance, and the horror of knowing she would soon be returned to her marionette shell, seemed to have canceled one another out. A chill spread through Penny, numbing her insides. There was no point in feeling emotions right now, or ever again. She had to do the right thing, but she didn't have to feel good or bad about it.

"The doors are all locked." Howard pushed on one for emphasis. Then he frowned and inspected it more closely. "Wait . . . this is painted on. How do we get in?"

Penny didn't answer, just walked around the trailer to the stage. She pulled herself up, then held out a hand to

Howard. They looked at the backdrop, the field of painted flowers, the fake sun and blue sky.

"What a pretty day," Penny said under her breath. She had been on this stage before.

Trailing her fingers along the screen, she followed it around to the darkness backstage. Howard stuck close behind her, accidentally kicking the backs of her shoes a few times. Penny stopped abruptly. They were sandwiched between the back of the screen and the wall of the trailer, with hardly enough room to turn around. Then, as her eyes adjusted, Penny saw the door. It was short and had no doorknob, but she could just make out the frame of it against the wall. Shuffling forward, Penny pressed her hand to the door and pushed.

It swung open, and behind her, Howard sighed in relief. Penny ducked under first. She straightened up, blinking in the dim light coming from a lantern. Howard followed suit and immediately cried: "Constance!"

At the sight of Constance's kind smile, Penny's eyes welled with tears. She hung her head, ashamed of herself for ever considering running off and stealing a body that was not hers. Perhaps she really was no better than a demon.

Seconds later Constance's arms were wrapped around her. "It's okay," she murmured, squeezing Penny tightly. "I knew you'd come back."

Hiccupping, Penny pulled away and tried to smile.

Then she noticed the marionettes, and her eyes widened in amazement.

Four sat on shelves just above a table. There was the Sheepherder, with a kind, freckled face, and the Brave Knight, with a helmet that covered everything but his maple-colored eyes. Below them sat the Evil Witch and the Wise Wizard, she with green painted wood and he with a silly white beard. Penny squinted and frowned. They had identical upturned noses and bright blue eyes.

"Striking, aren't they?"

The three children turned to find Fortunato standing there as if he'd appeared out of thin air. He was holding Princess Penny.

Before he could say a word, Constance crossed the room and snatched the marionette from his hands.

"My brother's in here," she said fiercely.

Fortunato sighed. "Yes, I know."

"You *know*." Constance glared at him, taking a step back and hugging the puppet close. "How long have you known? And why didn't you try to help? My brother trusted you, you know. So did I."

"Please listen." Fortunato closed his eyes, his voice low. "I'm sorry. I'm very sorry for allowing this to happen." He looked from Constance to Penny, his expression pleading. "I made a deal with the puppeteer. He wanted you and Chance to swap, and I went along with it because he . . . he has access to the cabinetmaker's chambers." Turning,

Fortunato gestured to the door of the spinning-wheel cabinet. "All of my papa's possessions are in there, things that are rightfully mine. But much more importantly—"

"You helped the puppeteer kidnap my brother in exchange for *things*?" Constance snapped.

"No." Fortunato's face drooped. "I helped him because he has Nicolette."

Penny's breathing grew shallow. "Who is Nicolette?"

"She's—"

"Not the concern of these children."

A chilly breeze blew through the trailer, and everyone turned to see the puppeteer in the doorway. Goose bumps rose on Penny's arms at the sight of him: the icy blue eyes, the unnaturally smooth, angled face, the spindly fingers. He met her gaze and smiled.

"Hello, Penny."

Penny did not respond. She glared defiantly at the puppeteer, her hands clenched into fists. But Constance spoke up, loud and confident.

"You horrible man," she spat, clutching the puppet in her arms even more tightly. "I don't know what you're trying to do, but it's too late. I'm taking my brother home, and Penny, too."

The puppeteer tilted his head. "Are you sure you want to take him in that state?"

"Very sure," Constance replied. "Penny and Chance can swap themselves back. A. P. Halls said as much."

221

"Oh no, I didn't mean his puppet state," the puppeteer said. "Fortunato?"

He held out his hand, and Fortunato, his face as gray as ash, hesitated only a moment before placing a single, shining string in his palm.

Penny's legs went wobbly. Fortunato had snipped the string off the marionette's head. Chance was lost in that fog, the same as she had been.

Constance noticed Penny's reaction, and her mouth set in a thin line. "Give me that string," she demanded.

"I could," the puppeteer said. "But it would do you little good without the spindle needed to reattach it. The magic is in the tools, as I'm sure you know. And I'm afraid that tool is no longer in your possession."

"Give it to us," Howard demanded. The puppeteer's eyes traveled over to him, and the corner of his mouth lifted.

"Ah," he said. "The Wright boy. I'd given up on you."

Howard's lips parted in a silent expression of confusion. Waving a hand dismissively, the puppeteer turned back to Penny.

"The spindle is where it belongs," he whispered. "On my spinning wheel. You may use it to swap with Chance— that is what you came here to do, is it not? So do it, and I'll allow the others into the chambers." He turned to Fortunato. "Nicolette is in there. She should be easy to find."

Fortunato moved toward the spinning-wheel cabinet. But the puppeteer blocked his path, looking expectantly at Penny.

He wanted her and Chance to swap back. But why?

Perhaps it didn't matter. After all, that was what Penny had come here to do.

She lifted her chin. "Fine," she said, hoping she sounded braver than she felt. "I'll do it."

Two bright pink spots appeared on Constance's cheeks. "I'll stay with you," she told Penny, but the puppeteer shook his head.

"I'm afraid that's not part of the deal."

"I'm not leaving my brother," Constance insisted.

The puppeteer smiled blandly. "Then, enjoy your puppet." He pocketed Chance's string, and Penny sighed.

"Let me do it alone," she told Constance. "Please."

Constance grimaced. "He'll lock us in there," she said. "You know he will."

"On the contrary," the puppeteer said. "We'll all enter the chambers together, and we'll leave together. You have my word."

With that, he pushed the door to the spinning-wheel cabinet open. The children gaped in astonishment.

Inside was an impossibly enormous chamber. Penny could make out archway after archway, room after room, extended infinitely like a trick with mirrors. The walls

223

were a series of cabinet doors of all shapes and sizes, made from every type of wood imaginable, all glowing as if by some internal magic.

The spinning wheel sat just on the other side of the door. Fortunato entered first, followed by the children, Constance still hugging the marionette close to her chest. The puppeteer closed the door behind them, then walked over to an enormous cast-iron stove in the corner. A few moments later, a bright, crackling fire was lit.

"It does get a bit drafty in here, doesn't it?"

This question was directed at Fortunato, who was glaring at the puppeteer.

"Where is she?" he said quietly, his voice quaking. "You promised."

The puppeteer gestured at the archway on Fortunato's left. "She's stored somewhere that way," he said, his tone detached, disinterested. "You should get started. This place is rather large, as you can see."

Fortunato set off immediately, and the puppeteer's cold eyes settled on Constance. She bit her lip, squeezing the marionette in her arms. Taking a deep breath, Penny stepped forward and held out her hands.

"Please," she said. "We have to do what he wants if we're going to save Chance."

"But . . ." Constance's voice cracked. "I don't trust him."

"Of course you don't," Penny said. "Villains aren't trustworthy. But look at it this way. Whatever the puppeteer is planning, Chance might know about it. We need him. Just . . . find Nicolette as fast as you can, and when you come back, he'll be here and the two of you will figure this out." She smiled at Constance. "This was the plan, right? Find Chance and swap back. And we're almost there."

Constance smiled too, but her eyes were red and watery. "Right." After a second's hesitation, she handed the marionette to Penny. Then she leaned close and whispered in Penny's ear: "Whatever he's up to, I won't leave you with him. I swear it."

Penny's throat was too tight to respond, so she just nodded. With one last glance at the marionette, Constance took Howard's hand, and they hurried after Fortunato. One tear slipped down Penny's cheek, then another.

Once the others were out of sight, the puppeteer removed the spindle from the spinning wheel. He handed it to Penny, along with a needle and the string.

"You know what to do," he said quietly.

Penny set the marionette carefully on the floor and took the gleaming tools. Clearly, the puppeteer had plans beyond Penny and Chance swapping back. And whatever those plans were, Penny was playing right into them. The Storm would never fall for this sort of trap.

But that was fiction, and this was reality. In reality, the Storm was an adult who told stories about how brave he was, but who had long forgotten what it meant to put others before himself. In reality, this was what Penny had come to do. To swap. To sacrifice. She could not imagine why the puppeteer had done any of this to begin with, nor could she imagine what he planned to do next. But she had to return Chance's soul to his body, where it belonged.

Taking a deep breath, Penny threaded the string through the needle. Then she wrapped the rest of the string around the spindle.

"Hold on, Fish Face. I'm coming."

The needle slipped easily under the marionette's scalp, and she pulled the string through. She pulled and pulled, and the spindle spun and spun, and soon the pulling was coming from the inside out, like something unraveling from within her, and as the trailer went dark, she finally realized what had been so obvious all along: she was giving away her soul, and it wasn't the first time.

HOLLOW WOODEN GIRL

The first thing Chance noticed was that his face was wet.

Waking up took too long, as if his mind wanted to keep him trapped in the nightmare he'd been having. He still hadn't managed to open his eyes. He just inhaled and exhaled and thought about how odd it was that he couldn't remember the details of his dream now, yet apparently it had been bad enough to make him cry in his sleep. He could only recall little bits and pieces. The feeling of being trapped. Claustrophobic. Controlled. Fog, and fog, and more fog. And the sight of his own face staring at him right before the nightmare finally ended.

But that wasn't me. That was Penny.

Chance's eyes flew open as the memories flooded back. The room spun around him, and he groaned. Every movement took far greater effort than it should have. First a finger. Then his hand, clenched into a weak fist. His arm, both arms, bracing against the floor as he lifted himself into a sitting position. Chance gulped in air like he hadn't breathed in days—which he hadn't, even if his body had. He wiped the cold trail of tears down his cheek, and his relief was quickly replaced with guilt and sadness. Because he had not cried these tears.

Penny had.

Through his blurred vision, he saw the giant cast-iron stove, the flames crackling and sparking inside. Gradually Chance became aware of another sound: a soft whirring noise behind him. With great effort, he twisted around to see the puppeteer sitting behind the spinning wheel, pumping the pedals.

"Just another minute," the puppeteer told Chance, his voice soft and calm. "I'm nearly ready."

Chance's heart began thumping too fast and too loud, and had he not been so terrified, he would have taken a moment to appreciate the sensation. The puppeteer was holding the dull severed string from the black box, and he was carefully winding it around the spindle. Something lay at his feet. No, not something. Someone.

"Penny," Chance whispered. But the second he reached for the marionette, the puppeteer made a soft *tsk* sound.

"Come now," he said, tapping the dull strings. "You peered inside my soul. I know you know what must be done, Chance. If you want to save her, there is only one way." The puppeteer stood, picked Penny up, and stepped aside. "Sit."

Chance swallowed, his eyes darting around the cavernous chambers with its cabinets made of glowing wood. Each and every door was closed, and he had no doubt that if he tried to open one, it would be locked. "Save her?" he repeated, glancing up at the puppeteer. "Are you saying that if I . . . if I do what you want, Penny won't be stuck like that forever?"

The puppeteer chuckled, and goose bumps broke out all over Chance's arms. "No. I'm afraid I cannot do a thing about Penny's current state," he said. "She's a marionette. But what I *can* do is promise she'll stay a marionette, rather than turning to ashes." And in one sudden, graceful movement, he swooped over to the cast-iron stove and held Penny in front of the open door. The flames crackled and spat behind her, and Chance scrambled to his feet with a cry.

"*Stop,*" the puppeteer hissed. "Listen to me. I cut off my soul and stored it in a box because I wasn't ready to die yet. I was old and scared, and I made the wrong choice, and now my body is . . ." He paused, flexing his brittle, twiglike fingers. "It's dying in a different way, I think. My soul needs a new body. One far from death. But this magic is about *giving,* not *taking.* I needed someone willing to make that sacrifice."

Chance looked up at the ceiling, down at his shoes, anywhere but at the dead-looking string.

"Fortunato gave me the idea, the poor man, though I don't think he meant to," the puppeteer went on, eyeing Chance greedily. "He begged me for years to return his puppet sister. He said he'd do *anything.* I realized if I could find another young boy willing to do anything to save his sibling, then I'd be saved as well. First I needed a new marionette. A child who was *sad.*"

The fire in the stove roared. Chance's palms began to sweat.

"Three times I failed," the puppeteer said. "The first boy had plenty of brothers, and I'm quite sure any of them would have sacrificed themselves to rescue him. But their parents kept them all locked up tight. Then there were the twins. That boy came the closest, but his sadness overpowered him and he ended up a puppet, a fool just like his sister. And Howard—well, Howard never managed to find Jack, thanks to the police getting in his way again and again."

Chance didn't understand any of this. He didn't want to. His legs were shaking uncontrollably.

"But I couldn't be too upset, because none of them was the *right* boy," the puppeteer whispered. "I thought I'd never find the *right* boy . . . and then I noticed you. I looked a lot like you, Chance, once upon a time. And you were Fortunato's apprentice, how perfect is that? I was once an apprentice, too, as I'm sure you've realized. I stole the old man's tools, the secret to his magic. I made that spinning wheel out of them." He shook Penny a bit, and Chance swallowed another cry. "It took some time to convince Fortunato to give Penny to you. He tried to convince me you wouldn't sacrifice yourself for her. I knew he was lying."

The puppeteer shook Penny again, holding her closer to the flames. Instinctively, Chance reached for her.

"How fascinating," the puppeteer murmured. "In the end, I didn't need siblings at all. You love her. And that's the bright side, Chance—isn't that what your family would say? You can be a hero. You can sit behind that wheel and do what must be done to save Penny . . . or you can watch her burn."

Chance's hands clenched at his sides. He imagined sitting behind the wheel, spinning the puppeteer's gray, rotten soul into his body, spinning out his own as shiny strings that would be locked in that little black box forever. For a brief moment, he considered refusing. Letting this demon throw Penny into the fire. She was just a puppet, after all.

Except she wasn't. Chance knew that now. But if he

told her, if he shouted the truth right now, surely the pup-peteer would feed her to the flames anyway.

There was only one option. It dawned on Chance that he'd spent his whole life preparing for the worst, like the Storm. But this was far, far worse than anything on a radio program. And he was not prepared at all.

He stumbled over to the spinning wheel, sat down, and placed his feet on the pedals. Penny had sacrificed herself for him, and now he would do the same for her. He had to.

Slowly Chance began to spin.

NICOLETTE

Constance glared at Fortunato's back. The man rushed from cabinet to cabinet with the eagerness of a schoolboy, and she hated him for it a little bit.

But the sooner they found Nicolette, the sooner they could get back to Chance and Penny. Once again Constance berated herself for leaving them with the puppeteer, but who knew what he would have done to Penny or Chance if Constance had disobeyed him? The glint in his pale eyes had made her skin crawl. So she opened one cabinet door after another as quickly as possible, eyes skimming over black opal tiaras and shiny compasses and jewel-encrusted swords before moving on to the next shelf.

"Constance!" Howard called, and she looked up just as Fortunato disappeared around the corner into yet another chamber. She ran to catch up with Howard, and they hurried to Fortunato's side.

"What are you doing?" she hissed, grabbing the man's arm. "We didn't check even close to every cabinet in that last room."

Fortunato quickly examined the contents of a cedar cabinet—thumb pianos, a giant conch shell, and a bright silver pan flute—then slammed the door.

"I know how Papa organized his collection," he cried, already hurrying across the room. "I lived here as a little boy; it's beginning to come back to me. Trust me—we don't have time to look in every single cabinet."

Constance and Howard exchanged a frustrated look before running after the former museum owner. Neither felt particularly inclined to trust him, but what choice did they have?

"Two more minutes," Constance told Howard under her breath. "Then we're going back to Penny and Chance, no matter what."

The boy nodded in agreement. They split off in different directions, moving around this new room in a circle, opening and closing cabinet doors as fast as they could. All the while, Fortunato muttered under his breath, and Constance could not tell whether he was talking to them or to himself.

"All these years, I thought this place had been destroyed in the fire. He told me Penny was the last of the marionettes. He gave me Penny and told me Nicolette had *burned,* that twisted demon. All these years, and she's been here the whole time. . . ."

Constance was barely listening; all her thoughts were of Penny and Chance, whether they had swapped back yet, what the puppeteer might want with them—and then she yanked open a yew cabinet and gasped.

A marionette hung by its strings from two hooks at the top of the cabinet. A girl, fair-haired, with storm-cloud eyes and cheeks as pink as if she'd just come inside from the cold. She was taller than Constance, and her white dress was an old-fashioned style, with a wide collar and a pale pink sash that hung low on her waist.

"Oh!"

Constance stepped aside when Fortunato appeared, one hand over his mouth. Howard hurried over too, eyes wide.

"Nicolette," Fortunato whispered, gently lifting one string, then another, off their hooks. "I can't believe it. At last . . ."

"Good," Constance said, taking a step back. "We found your doll. Now can we—"

"This is no doll." Fortunato's voice was nearly reverent

235

as he carefully removed the marionette from her cabinet. "This is my sister."

"Your . . . *what?*"

Tears filled his eyes as he held her strings. "Yes, it's me," he whispered, and Constance realized he was talking to the marionette. *With* the marionette. "I'm so sorry, Nicolette. He took you while I was sleeping."

Constance's mouth opened and closed. "Okay," she said at last, taking Howard's hand. "Come on, we don't need him."

Blinking rapidly, Fortunato looked at Constance. He clutched Nicolette to his chest, and though it was absurd, Constance thought she actually saw a resemblance between them.

An awful image flashed in her mind. Herself, old and wrinkled like Fortunato, still searching for her lost brother trapped in a marionette. A fresh wave of adrenaline coursed through her veins at the thought. She had to get back to Chance. *Now.*

"We lost our parents to pneumonia when we were very little," Fortunato was saying. "The cabinetmaker took us in, treated us like we were his own. Until . . ."

He closed his eyes, and Constance felt her patience snap.

"We don't have time for this right now! We need to save Penny and Chance."

"No, listen!" Fortunato stepped forward, his gray eyes now wide with alarm. "I can help both of you save your brothers. Yes, Jack, too," he added to Howard, whose mouth was a round O of surprise. "But if we're going to defeat the puppeteer, you need to know the truth about him."

Constance and Howard shared a nervous look. Howard nodded, and Constance took a deep breath, fighting the instinct to sprint back to Chance as fast as she could. She couldn't act rashly. She needed a plan.

"Tell us."

36

THUMP-THUMP

Penny could not feel the flames just inches from her back, but she could hear them crackling. Her glass eyes were aimed right at Chance as he spun his soul away. She wanted to scream at him to stop, stop that *right now*. Why should both of their souls be trapped forever, when they could both be free? She willed Chance to understand this, to let the puppeteer throw her into the fire. But he just kept spinning.

He's doing what he thinks is right, came the puppeteer's voice in her mind. *Just like you did, coming back here to save him. Sacrificing. Giving.*

Penny did not respond. She focused on Chance.

His eyes were glazing over, his movements stiffening. He seemed mesmerized by the wheel. Penny understood why. There was something about the blur of the spokes. She'd been hypnotized by them too once before.

Wait, no, she hadn't. She'd never sat behind that spinning wheel. But then why could she imagine it so vividly? Sinking into an emotionless fog, her pain and sadness ebbing away (What pain? What sadness? *Lottie . . .*), the magic of seeing that first shining bit of string appear out of nowhere . . . no, not out of nowhere, out of *herself*, spinning straw into gold, souls into strings . . . the joints of her fingers and wrists and elbows tautening, her brown skin hardening into wood, nicking her chin on that long, sharp spindle and barely feeling it . . .

Sounds like a fairy tale, the puppeteer said, jarring her from these thoughts. *Just like Princess Penny, foolishly drinking the Evil Witch's potion. She makes the wrong choice every time.*

Because you force her to, Penny thought, the fog in her mind receding rapidly now. *That's the way you tell the story when you're holding her strings. But that isn't how it has to go. Lottie . . .* Constance, *Constance will stop you.*

And just as she thought Constance's name, the girl appeared. Penny could barely make her out from the corners of her glass eyes, edging around the outskirts of the chamber toward the entrance to the trailer. Howard was right behind her, his gaze locked on the puppeteer.

Oh, she won't know, the puppeteer assured her, too fixated on Chance to notice the others' return. *Once my soul has a new home, this body will no longer work. She'll come in to find that Chance has triumphed—the puppeteer will be dead wood on the floor, and her brother will be returned to his normal state. We will all leave these chambers together, as I promised.*

She'll know, Penny told him. Constance and Howard had nearly reached the door, and she willed the puppeteer not to turn his head. *Constance will know who you are the second she looks into her brother's eyes. She did with me.*

The puppeteer did not answer. Constance and Howard had vanished from Penny's view, and she waited. They must have seen what Chance was doing; surely they had a plan to stop him, to save him.

Suddenly, music began playing on the other side of the door. Fortunato's radio was turned on full blast, and *Live from Club Heavenly Blues* had begun. The singer's voice, a bit hoarse from age but still sweet, filled Penny with yet another surge of emotions. And then, in her chest:

Thump.

Penny felt the puppeteer's shock as much as she felt her own. He held her closer to the fire and yelled at Chance, "Spin faster!"

Thump-thump.

Her heart was beating.

You're delusional, the puppeteer hissed. *You're a marionette; you don't have a heart. You're nothing but wood and a bit of string.*

240

But his lies didn't faze Penny. She'd spun out her soul once long ago, not because she was foolish, but because she was very, very sad and didn't want to feel anything anymore. And then she'd forgotten who she was, almost entirely. But now she remembered.

Time slowed as Fortunato appeared, carrying a fair-haired marionette. Constance and Howard burst back into the chambers with the radio, music echoing around the cavernous hall. They were shouting something, saying Penny's name. But Penny did not hear them. For a moment, she didn't even see them.

She saw Lottie and Walter.

Walter, her brother who'd died in a war fought across the ocean. Lottie, who fell into a deep depression that made her a beloved singer but a neglectful sister. It was very, very long ago, but Penny remembered it all now. They'd lost their parents, but Walter and Lottie had raised her. They were musicians, they were happy, they were a family until the war changed everything, stole it all away. And so Penny had run off. Snuck into a trailer that glowed with promised magic. Sat behind an enchanted spinning wheel. Spun out her soul.

I want it back, Penny thought, and her chest went *thump-thump. I want to spin my soul back in.*

"You can't," the puppeteer snapped, loud and angry. "You need the cabinetmaker's tools. Only the tools have the magic to—"

"It's not the tools!" Fortunato yelled with a look of fury Penny had never seen on his kind face. "He told you that again and again, but you never listened."

The puppeteer let out a harsh laugh. "Oh yes, the ridiculous idea that the magic was in the wood. A pathetic attempt to keep the secret of his success from his apprentice."

But Fortunato was not looking at him. He was looking at Penny.

"The tools aren't magical, Penny. They're just tools."

The tools are everything. The puppeteer spoke only in her mind, and he sounded desperate now. *You're just a puppet. A thief. A demon jealous of real children with souls.*

No, Penny thought. *I am not a thief. I am not a demon.* The love and sorrow she felt from the memories washing over her were agonizing, and she welcomed them. Her heart thumped and her lungs inhaled and her strings retracted and her mouth moved and she *spoke.*

"I am a *person.*"

The spinning wheel stopped spinning. Chance gazed at her, and already his eyes seemed less cloudy, as if he were coming out of a deep trance. Fortunato laughed triumphantly, still clutching Nicolette. Constance and Howard dropped the radio in shock, bringing the music to an abrupt end.

The puppeteer gripped Penny's arms tighter than ever, his perfectly carved face contorted in rage.

"Flesh can burn as easily as wood," he hissed, and pushed her at the oven door.

But Penny braced her legs against the iron and pushed back with all her strength. The flames from the oven licked her back, singeing her hair. All she could see was the puppeteer's face, his nose nearly touching hers. Up close she could see all the strange little scars from where he'd carved his wrinkles away as decades passed.

Penny did not scream, but she heard cries of anger over the fire crackling in her ears. A pair of hands grabbed the puppeteer's shoulders, another took his left arm, and another his right. Constance and Howard and Fortunato pulled as hard as they could, but the puppeteer was too strong. Penny's calves were starting to burn from pressing against the hot iron, and her muscles, which had gone so long unused, would not last much longer. The puppeteer's lips curled back in a sneer.

But Penny was not looking at him anymore. Because Chance was standing just behind him. Not pulling or yelling like the others. Just staring at Penny with a question in his eyes.

And even though it was impossible, because neither of them was a marionette anymore, Penny heard him ask:

What should I do?

And she answered him:

Push.

Chance did not hesitate. He shoved his shoulder into the puppeteer's back just as Penny threw herself to the side with the last bit of strength she had. Fortunato stumbled away, and Constance and Howard let go of the puppeteer in surprise.

He flew face-first into the fire in a clatter of wooden limbs. Constance kicked the door closed, then covered her mouth with her hands, shocked by her own actions. The four children and the former museum owner stared at the oven.

They listened and listened, but the puppeteer did not scream.

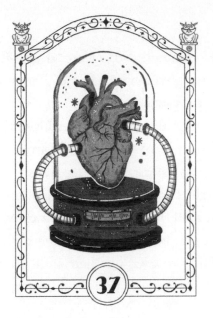

SOMEWHERE IN THAT FOG

Soft music crackled from the radio, filling the trailer with rhythmic swing and an upbeat melody. There were five people and five marionettes, and none of them were sure what to do next.

"There has to be a way to change them back," Howard said, his palms resting on either side of Jack's cheeks. He had not taken his eyes off his brother's face since removing the knight's helmet, which had kept it hidden.

Constance was busily cleaning the green paint off the witch's face. "The puppeteer tricked them into forgetting who they are," she said, lifting one of the witch's strings. "She told me she doesn't have a name. They all think they're just these silly fairy-tale characters."

Next to her, Chance carefully removed the white beard from the wizard's face. "These two look alike," he said. "Like brother and sister."

"They could be," Fortunato murmured, turning the black box that held the puppeteer's strings over and over in his hands. "He was looking for children with brothers who would be willing to give up their souls to save their siblings. It takes a particularly powerful love to drive someone to make such a sacrifice."

At this, Chance's face went red as a beet, and he busied himself examining the white beard so closely it looked as though he were inspecting it for lice.

Penny, still dazed and unable to believe she was really standing here, moving and talking in her own body, stared at the coil of dull string on the table. It was all that remained of the puppeteer, and none of them knew what to do with it now. Penny had been the one to collect it off the spindle. When she'd touched it, there had been no voice in her head.

The door opened suddenly, and everyone turned to see A. P. Halls, out of breath and flustered-looking. His eyes traveled across their faces, and the faces of the marionettes.

"The puppeteer . . . ," he choked out, and Penny pointed wordlessly to the coil of string.

"Gone," said Fortunato.

"As you can see, Mr. Halls," Constance said primly, "it wasn't too late after all."

The young man's face turned slightly pink. "Indeed."

"Halls?" Chance yelped, and Penny couldn't help but smile. His mouth was doing the fish thing again. "You're . . . you're the Storm!"

Constance muttered something under her breath that sounded like "Hardly."

As Fortunato began to recount the incident in the chambers to Mr. Halls, Penny returned her attention to the Wise Wizard and the Evil Witch. *Twins,* she thought vaguely, and then her eyes moved to the Brave Knight, and to the Sheepherder, and to Fortunato's sister. Sadness had led them to spin out their souls, and now they thought they were just marionettes. But it wasn't too late. The real story was still inside each of them, lost somewhere in that fog. Penny had found her real story. She could help them find theirs.

"The marionettes are *children*?" Mr. Halls cried. His fish face was almost as funny as Chance's. "But . . . but how do we help them?"

"Finally, the right question," Constance said, but her expression had softened considerably. "And I think Penny might have the answer."

Penny stood a little taller. "I think I might too."

The others fell silent as she stepped forward. Gently she touched the string on the Brave Knight's wrist.

Hello? came a boy's voice.

"Hello, Jack," Penny said. "I'm going to tell you the story of how you became a marionette."

ENOUGH HAPPY ENDINGS

Early the next morning, the rain clouds that had hung so low over the city drifted away at last, and the sun rose bright and strong.

What a pretty day, thought Mrs. Goldstein, sipping bitter black coffee on her balcony. She enjoyed watching the city come to life this early in the morning and was grateful she and her husband had decided not to move to Daystar Meadows, no matter how many reminders their home held of what they'd lost. Just down the street, she noticed a boy and a girl dressed in silly costumes—a witch and a wizard—and she laughed to herself even as her heart constricted with sadness. Then the children saw her and waved and yelled and started to run, and Mrs. Goldstein knocked over her coffee mug in shock, and she screamed for Mr. Goldstein as she barreled through the apartment and down the stairs and down the street toward her grandchildren.

What a pretty day, thought Sister Maria Ignacia as the sunbeams shone through the stained-glass windows. She was once again the first to arrive for morning prayer, and she had been struck with déjà vu as soon as she'd entered the church. Instinctively, she glanced over at the first pew, and for a moment, she thought she was imagining the boy in brown robes curled up there, sound asleep. Sister Maria Ignacia had not been able to forget the brother and sister who had slept there the night before last, and she had added them to her prayers. But this was not the same boy. She knew this boy, and he was not lost anymore. "Gil?" she whispered, and her nephew opened his eyes and smiled, and Sister Maria Ignacia fell to her knees because this was the miracle she'd been praying for.

What a pretty day, thought Mrs. Pepperton as she picked up the newspaper on the orphanage's porch. She skimmed the headlines with a sigh before rolling the paper up and sticking it under her arm. Across the street, a pair of boys emerged from the park. Mrs. Pepperton frowned, because she recognized Howard right away—the boy had snuck off again, heaven help her. Then she took a closer look at the smaller boy. He was wearing what appeared to be a suit of armor, a helmet tucked under his arm. He waved when he saw her, and he and Howard wore identical smiles. Mrs. Pepperton took an involuntary step forward, hardly daring to believe her eyes. "Jack," she murmured. "Oh, Jack. He found you."

The chief of police had a busy morning. But it was one of those rare kinds of busy in a police station when the phone kept ringing with good news, not bad. The Goldsteins' grandkids had returned. So had the missing Espinosa boy. Mrs. Pepperton was his third call, and she informed him, her voice thick with tears, that Howard had found his brother, Jack, as well.

Pleased but perplexed, the chief hung up the phone. He would have to question all these children later. They had each vanished without a trace, and now they were all back at the same time—it was too good to be true. And yet as he opened his office door, he couldn't help but wish for one more stroke of luck.

"I'm sorry to keep you waiting, Mr. and Mrs. Bonvillain," he said.

The couple stood, their hands clasped tightly. The chief took a deep breath. Their children had sat on that very bench just a day ago, and then they'd vanished as well. He'd had his officers out searching for them all night, with no luck. And now he had to deliver the bad news.

But just as he opened his mouth, the bells over the entrance jangled. The chief and the Bonvillains turned to look. And like something out of a fairy tale, the missing brother and sister walked right into the police station.

There were tears of relief and hugging and halfhearted threats of punishment that the chief felt sure would not be carried out. He watched the reunion with no small degree of incredulity. And then he noticed the others hanging back by the door. An elderly man with gray hair, holding the hand of a blond girl the chief assumed was his grand-daughter. And a younger man, slim and well dressed, holding the hand of a blue-haired girl the chief assumed was his daughter.

There was a third girl too, but she was alone. She wore an old-fashioned dress smudged with what looked like soot. A scar marred her chin, and a few of her fingers were merely stubs. A tiara sat atop her head, and her dark curls were pulled into a messy, knotted braid. She was the saddest princess the police chief had ever seen.

The Bonvillains had not noticed the others yet. They could not seem to take their eyes off their children's faces, as if they'd never properly looked at them before, and now they never wanted to stop.

But eventually Mr. Bonvillain glanced over at the

elderly man. "Fortunato!" he exclaimed in surprise. "What are you doing here?"

His wife looked up too, and she let out a little squeak at the sight of the princess. Her son rushed to the girl's side and grabbed her mangled hand, and his sister joined them.

"This is Penny," Chance announced, and Mrs. Bonvillain squeaked again.

Mr. Bonvillain blinked several times. "Your . . . doll?"

"Marionette," Constance corrected him. "But not anymore."

The chief of police cleared his throat. "If you don't mind, I have some questions for you children."

He spent nearly three hours writing down their story. Sister Maria Ignacia arrived with Gil just after lunch, and Mrs. Pepperton brought in Howard and Jack not long after. When the Goldsteins arrived with Linda and Lyle, Constance promptly burst into tears and hugged Mrs. Goldstein as if she were her own grandmother.

By sunset the chief had compiled the strangest report of his career. He wasn't entirely sure he believed it, and he knew the other adults felt the same way.

"I think I can prove it," Penny told them.

And so they followed her, a procession out of the police station and up the street. The conversation was lively as they walked block after block, into a neighborhood that hadn't yet changed like the rest of the city. The stars

253

began to twinkle overhead as the sky faded from blue to black.

Nerves gnawed at Penny's stomach. Not all endings were happy, like the Storm always said. Chance and Constance, Jack and Howard, Gil and Nicolette, Linda and Lyle—they'd been reunited with their families, and she was glad for that. But Penny wasn't sure there were enough happy endings to go around.

She was not a demon, though, and not a marionette. She was a person. And that was certainly more than she'd ever dared dream. No one would ever hold her strings again.

The chatter fell silent when the group stopped in front of Club Heavenly Blues. The marquee, now flashing and bright, read LIVE! THE CHARLOTTE BELL TRIO, and the sound of saxophone and piano and drums leaked out onto the street. And a voice, that beautiful voice still achingly familiar despite decades of age, singing Penny's favorite song:

"Every time it rains, it rains pennies from heaven. . . ."

"I hope Lottie remembers me," Penny whispered, eyes already welling up. It was so easy to forget, after all.

"She will," Chance said emphatically. "I know it."

Penny wiped her eyes and smiled. "Thanks, Fish Face," she said, and he blushed.

Constance took her hand, and Chance took her other hand, and the three of them walked into the club together.

The music washed over Penny, and her gaze went straight to the singer onstage, drinking in every detail of her beautifully wrinkled face. Their eyes met, and Penny's soul twirled and soared.

She was home.

Acknowledgments

When a storm—or a book—is brewing, it's important to surround yourself with people who can help you prepare for the worst. This novel would have been a disaster without . . .

My editor and Wise Wizard, Diane Landolf, and everyone on the Random House Children's team, who uncovered the real story beneath all the false versions I wrote first.

My agent and Brave Knight, Sarah Davies, who constantly saves me from drinking the green potion.

My illustrator, Kathrin Honesta, and designer, Leslie Mechanic, the incredible Princesses who brought Penny and Chance to life in these pages.

My beta readers and friends Alison Cherry, Claire Legrand, Lindsay Ribar, and Kaitlin Ward. You are all, of course, the most Evil Witches.

The year 2016, during which I wrote the first draft of this book. Thank you for teaching me the real meaning of pessimism and for instilling in me the belief that all Puppeteers eventually fall.

And lastly, the Sheepherders. You know who you are.